ALFIE'S ADVENTURES

Book 2

Gerald Howe

Pen Press Publishers Ltd

Second edition 2006

First published in Great Britain
Pen Press Publishers Ltd
39 Chesham Rd
Brighton BN2 1NB

ISBN 1 905203-20-9

A catalogue record for this book is available
from the British Library

Printed and bound in Great Britain

Cover design by Jacqueline Abromeit
Illustrations by Channimation

About the Author

Gerald Howe was born in Bedford in 1954 to a family of farmers and cattle dealers. He went to Bedford Modern School and represented England at rowing.

Happily married to Jacqueline since 1976, the couple have two sons, Mathew and Henry, and a black Labrador called Eddie!

Gerald has worked at various airports including Heathrow where he looked after the in-flight catering of Qantas, Gulf Air and TWA Airlines. He later became a restaurateur and then a hotelier, and moved to Jersey in the Channel Islands in 1988.

Though actively involved in an electronics business in Bedford, in his spare time he sat down at his computer and started to write the Alfie stories . . . which he hopes will give children a sense of adventure and an interest in reading.

Foreword

Calling all potential heroes!

Roman emperors, jungle explorers, maps to find hidden treasures and lost cities and plans to save the Earth from pollution – exactly what you wouldn't expect to find on board a Virgin flight.

But look within these pages to join Alfie and his faithful dog Eddie as they time travel around the world to different places and times, being an action hero in the past, present and future.

Best of all, Alfie's night-time adventures seem to be giving him heroic powers during the day as he catches criminals, saves a man from drowning and to top it all, beats the school bully at his own game.

So, settle back into your Virgin seat AS IT MAY BE WORTH YOUR WHILE TO LEARN what you would do if…

… you need to rescue a diver from the tentacles of an octopus

… you have to winch a trapped man out of the quicksand

… you find yourself drifting into outer space whilst repairing your space rocket

… you need to put out a fire on a three hundred foot high drilling rig

… or you merely have to reclaim your tree-house from the school bullies!

Read on to find out how to be a hero and enjoy!

Best Wishes

Gerald Howe

PS. See how smart you are. Every picture has a Virgin "V" hidden within it. Can you find them all?

ALFIE'S ADVENTURES

Book 2

Special Edition Lunch Box Set

Books 1 to 4

ISBN 1-905621-58-2

The story so far…

Alfie has been experiencing the most extraordinary night-time adventures ever since his antique-collector Grampy shipped a bed home for him from one of his travels abroad.

When Grampy arrived unexpectedly in Bombay, he discovered that all the hotel rooms were full - except for a tiny room in the farthest reaches of a small ramshackle hotel in the heart of the bustling, colourful city. The bed in it was too small but, Grampy HAD no choice than to take what he was offered.

That night, he was so comfortable and he had such dreams! The next day the hotel owner told him that the bed had chosen him! This mysterious man said that he must buy the ornate bed; he was most insistent and sold it to him very cheaply. Grampy, being a collector; was only too keen to comply and had the bed shipped back to England for his grandson, Alfie Nelson.

Alfie loved the bed immediately. Both ends of the bed had dark wooden slats, and on each corner was an ornate post topped with temptingly smooth round spheres. Upon closer investigation, Alfie noticed that the carvings on the bed posts were comprised of letters and numbers. A far more exciting bed than his last one – particularly as he started having the most amazing time-travelling adventures.

His night-time travels take him to weird and wonderful parts of the world – battling pirates on the Caribbean seas and fighting bandits in medieval Britain; Alfie finds lost treasures and cities whilst rescuing damsels in distress.

But was he only dreaming, or were these adventures really happening to him? The little mementoes under his pillow each morning were certainly real enough – and Alfie's daytime adventures mirror his nighttime adventures, rapidly making him a twenty-four hour a day hero!

At the end of Book 1, Alfie had found some very old and valuable Roman coins in Farmer Appleton's field. The reward from the British Museum had resulted in Alfie getting a brand new bike AND a holiday in Antigua...

Chapter One
Tripping Over The Keys

Alfie's alarm woke him up with a start as he realized that THIS was the day he was going on HOLIDAY to Antigua. It was FIVE o'clock in the morning! He had hardly slept all night as he thought about the three hundred and sixty five beaches waiting to be explored.

He leapt out of bed and thundered down the stairs to let Eddie - his black Labrador retriever - out into the back garden. Eddie nearly knocked Alfie over in the rush to get out of the door. He was in a big rush because there was the big tabby cat from next door in his garden!

Alfie's dad came down to make a cup of tea and find out what the commotion was all about. He laughed when he saw the cat sitting on the top of the fence looking all superior and detached, whilst Eddie, who was trying to jump up, was barking his head off!

"Come on in boy! Let that cat alone, we've got a lot on today," said Alfie's dad.

Eddie scampered in reluctantly and positioned himself near the cooker from where he would be able to beg for a sausage at breakfast time.

After getting dressed, Alfie's mum cooked them a huge breakfast. "Humm, just the job for hungry explorers to eat before setting out on their expedition," said Alfie.

Eddie had just begged a piece of sausage off everyone at the table when the front doorbell rang. Alfie dashed to open the door - it was Grampy and Gran.

"Hello you young rascal, have you got a hug for your old Grampy? I know that you are too big for a kiss now!"

Alfie was swept up in the arms of his Gran, who grabbed him first and gave him a big smacker on the cheek. Alfie hadn't seen his grandparents for several months as they lived a long way away but he had often spoken to them on the phone. The reason they lived so far apart was because Alfie's Dad had changed to a better job and they had to move to be nearer his work.

Gran and Grampy had come to look after Eddie whilst Alfie, his Mum and Dad went on holiday. Alfie's Mum had left a long list of Eddie's requirements, detailing such things as walks and treats after walks. At lunchtime Eddie was to have tuna and Eukanuba followed by an afternoon walk and treats. Then dinner of a small tin of co-op mince and onions and Eukanuba. Before bed, Eddie also had a piece of thickly buttered toast... oh, and of course, fresh water in his bowl with a few ice cubes.

Grampy laughed when he saw the list, "You treat him like a little prince," he said.

Alfie's Dad had started to load the suitcases into the back of the car. Alfie had tied a big red and yellow band around each of the cases. He did this so that the cases could be spotted easily as they went round the baggage system at the airport.

Pretty soon Alfie's grandparents were settled in. They had found Eddie's lead and after the family had left for the airport, they were planning to take him for a walk. Alfie hugged Eddie goodbye, sat in the car and did up his seatbelt. Everybody waved as they set off for Gatwick Airport.

After about half an hour of travelling Alfie was becoming impatient, "Are we there yet, Dad?" he asked.

"No. About another half hour and we will be," his Dad replied.

Alfie's Mum gave him the map to check as they went along.

This kept Alfie occupied as he checked that his Dad was going the right way.

They arrived at Gatwick where the roadsigns became very confusing, pointing them this way and that way... They were fortunate that they had Alfie the explorer with them, as he guided them into the Long Term Car Park. "Well done Alfie," said his Dad as he pulled into the car park. They unloaded the car and had to wait for a shuttle bus to take them into the Departures Hall.

They soon found the Virgin Atlantic check-in desks which were situated at the far end. People were queuing up for check-in, snaking line by line and only divided by aisles made of red ropes. They slowly shuffled forward, gradually getting closer and closer, until it was their turn to be checked in for their flight to Antigua.

Alfie's Dad got their tickets and passports out to show to the lady in the smart red uniform. She weighed the cases then labelled them up before giving them their boarding cards. Alfie watched as the lady pressed a button and the cases zoomed off one by one down a baggage conveyor belt. He thought that it looked like a fun way to travel.

Then they all went to a security gate and had their boarding cards checked and their hand baggage X-rayed in a machine.

Alfie's Mum's make-up bag was searched as the X-ray showed all sorts of shapes that the security lady spotted and had to check, to make sure it was safe to travel. Even Alfie bleeped when he went through the scanner gate. A security man asked him to hold out his arms and he searched him. Inside Alfie pocket was the large silver button he had been given by aliens in one of his earlier adventures.

Alfie frowned and thought, "That's funny. I don't remember packing that!" The security man also frowned as he looked at it, shrugged and gave it back.

Alfie was free to explore the duty free shopping area. They went to the bookshop and bought a few books for the holiday because all Alfie's Mum wanted to do, was sit in the sun on the beach with a book and get a good tan. Alfie was checking the departure screens when he saw that their flight VS033 was called as boarding at gate 72.

The family set off on the way to the gate and rode on the moving walkways. Alfie looked at all the different aircraft on the stands as they went past. It looked like all the people in the world were travelling that day!

The gate was a long way and when they arrived they found the jumbo was being boarded by seat row numbers. They waited a few minutes because their seats were in the middle of the plane. The airhostess showed them to their seats and she offered Alfie a Virgin Kids pack to keep him occupied.

Alfie was soon reading about the TV screen controls and how to get the kid's channel.

The hubbub of boarding passengers soon died down and the doors shut and the engines started. "Bang on time Dad. Ten thirty," announced Alfie, as he checked his watch. The Jumbo was pushed back onto the taxiway by a big powerful tug. Alfie watched out of the window as a man in headphones walked away from the push back and hitched a ride with the tug driver.

The aircrew did a safety demonstration as the jumbo taxied out towards the runway.

This took nearly twenty minutes as the jumbo waited for a turn to take off. Alfie thought that the plane was going to taxi all the way to Antigua! The engines roared as the jumbo thundered down Gatwick's main runway. The nose lifted off and Alfie felt the whole plane take off up into the air.

The force pressed him back into his seat. The front of the plane was at a very steep angle. 'Though not as steep as when I climbed Everest,' thought Alfie.

Alfie undid the pack with the earphones in and started

playing with the TV screen and looking at the various channels. His Mum and Dad just relaxed with a coffee and Alfie had an orange juice.

"Settle down young man. It's a long flight," advised his Mum. "It is longer than a whole day at school."

"Really?" Alfie's eyes widened in surprise as he looked around the space that was to be where he would have to sit for the next 8 hours.

"That's why you have so much to entertain you," said mum, pointing to his little TV and kid's activity pack. He decided to investigate his kid's pack and whiled away some time reading, colouring and playing with its contents. He decided he would keep the bag for his school things.

Alfie looked out of the window and watched the land below until it all became just sea. The clouds were very bright with the sun and soon all was a blanket of white and golden pillows floating by. Alfie felt quite tired after his early morning start. He wondered how Eddie was getting on – and grinned to himself when he thought that Eddie was probably taking Gran and Grampy for a walk!

Lunch was brought round on trays and Alfie took great care in opening and sampling all the individual portions of food. Later a hostess gave him an ice cream lolly, which Alfie ate as he settled back to watch Shrek 2 on his screen for the next couple of hours. 'I'm really enjoying this holiday already,' he thought happily, his eyelids already beginning to droop. His mother noticed him yawning, and suggested that he take a bit of a nap. Alfie snuggled down with a couple of pillows and a blanket. He felt in his pocket and held the silver button gently as his eyelids closed shut.

Eddie bounded down the front garden and sat patiently by the gate waiting for Grampy and Gran to take him for his evening walk. Grampy locked the front door behind him and, as he went to put the lead on Eddie, he accidentally dropped the keys into the flowerbed alongside the path – but he didn't notice them fall.

They walked down the road and into the park. Grampy let Eddie off the lead and he ran into the trees sniffing each one. Gran sat on the bench while Grampy ambled along behind the dog. And the strange thing is that Alfie could see all of this in his dream - as if he were there but not there, if that makes sense?

The daylight was fading when they returned to the house. Grampy felt into his pocket for the keys but couldn't find them. "Oh dear! What are we going to do now?" he said to Gran. "I could have lost them anywhere."

Alfie wanted to tell them that he had seen the keys being dropped into the flowerbed. Then he thought of Eddie's favourite game of burying the bone and then looking for it. He concentrated very hard and told Eddie to seek. Eddie pricked up his ears, looked left and right as if puzzled by something then took off round the garden and started sniffing. Go left, thought Alfie. Go forward, now right, further into the bushes, just around there… that's it! Eddie's snout dug into the flowers and he emerged with the keys delicately held between his big crocodile jaws.

"Give them to Grampy," thought Alfie. Eddie dropped the keys on top of Grampy's feet. "What a clever dog!" said Grampy. A great sigh of relief was heard from Gran.

The door closed shut with a loud click and Alfie woke up back in the jumbo, as his Mum was buckling up her seat belt ready for landing.

Alfie took the silver button from his pocket and noticed that it had turned black because it was now out of charge. 'But I used it to good effect,' thought Alfie. 'I hope it recharges itself soon.'

Chapter Two
Watch Out For The Green Flash!

The jumbo pulled on to its stand at V.C.Bird Airport in Antigua. The ground crew drove a set of steps up to the side of the aircraft as fuel tankers, baggage, catering and cleaners trucks besieged the newly arrived jet.

It had taken about nine hours for the flight from London yet due to the time difference it was about two o'clock in the afternoon in Antigua. Alfie strapped his smart new red Virgin bag onto his back and made his way to the doors of the aeroplane. Alfie was taken aback as a blast of very hot air engulfed him as he stood at the top of the steps, and he clambered down past the big engines mounted on the wing – with even more heat radiating from there.

"Hot enough for you?" said Dad, mopping his brow.

They were all put on a big coach that bent in the middle and taken to the small terminal building. The terminal was quite a change from Gatwick. They had to form a queue to see an immigration officer who checked Alfie's passport; the man winked at Alfie and waved him through to the baggage hall. The passengers all stood waiting at the one belt as their bags came slowly round. Alfie looked anxiously, hoping that his bag would soon appear. Eventually all three bags arrived safely and Alfie helped his Dad load them on to a trolley.

They breathed a sigh of relief as they got onto the cool air-conditioned coach, escaping the heat of the hot afternoon sun. They were sitting near the front, and the driver chatted away to them, pointing out features of interest as they went along the road from the airport to the Hawksbill Hotel. It was called this because of a huge rock, just offshore, that was shaped like a Hawksbill turtle's head.

They checked in and were shown to a garden chalet room that was about twenty yards from a long thin sandy beach. They plonked the bags down, ordered themselves some drinks at the poolside bar and went and sat in the shade of the big palm trees. They took in the wonderful view and blessed the day that Alfie had found the roman coins in Farmer Appleton's field. The holiday was paid for by part of the treasure trove cheques that Alfie and his Dad had been given by the British Museum.

"Let's have a toast to Alfie," said his mum, raising her iced coke. They all clinked glasses and cheered each other.

After a refreshing shower they attended The Manager's Welcome Party. Alfie's Mum and Dad each enjoyed a big rum punch. Alfie had a large orange juice with a small umbrella in it.

They were soon chatting to the other guests. One guest, who had been there before, started to tell them about the various trips they could go on. Alfie liked the sound of the round island boat trip. They sat chatting and soon it was about seven o'clock. The sun went down and then disappeared in a final green flash of light.

At about eight o'clock they went to have dinner in a really beautiful dining room, which overlooked the sea. The sides were open and the gentle sea breeze blew through the restaurant. Alfie really enjoyed the food but his eyes were drooping so his Mum put him to bed – after all, with the time difference it was really midnight in his body clock. She kissed him goodnight then joined his Dad on the veranda; looking at the galaxies of stars in the clear night sky.

Alfie was first up next morning and within five minutes of being awake he had dragged his Mum and Dad into the warm sea with him for a quick pre-breakfast swim. He thought it was strange waking up without his pal Eddie greeting him and he hoped he was getting on all right.

After a breakfast of eggs and very crisp bacon, Alfie decided to explore the beach and its surroundings. He wandered down near the main hotel entrance and noticed about ten children playing cricket on the beach. He sat down watching them, when a ball flew in his direction. He jumped up and caught it with a flying dive to his right. He landed in the sand and ended up with a face full of gritty sand. The other kids cheered as he had just caught out their star batsman. They asked if he wanted to play and soon he was fielding on the beach with his feet in several inches of water. A bit different from home he thought.

Alfie's Mum watched them play. Occasionally she called him over to have sun lotion rubbed over him. Alfie's Mum was talking to a lady who was painting a bright picture of the boys playing cricket and the beach behind them. Alfie noticed how much his Mum liked the lady's pictures.

At lunchtime it was so hot that they all sat in the shade and drank cold cans of lemonade and cola from a beach café. The place was a bit different to the beach café at home, where Alfie's Mum worked at the weekends.

Alfie's new mates encouraged him to try some of the dishes. He liked the jerk chicken but when the lads gave him a small spoonful of rice with hot sauce on it, he turned red and started coughing with his mouth on fire. They all laughed, as he drunk two cans of lemonade before the fire in his mouth became calm enough to bear.

That afternoon he went snorkelling. Just offshore under the water was a reef that had loads of tiny fish swimming in and around it. Later that day, he tried to canoe but he kept falling out. Alfie was not the sort of person that gets defeated easily, so he kept on trying until he mastered it.

That evening at dinner, his Dad told them that he had some tickets for the round island catamaran tour for the next day, and it was a very excited Alfie who half-ran to the Jolly Harbour the next morning where they boarded a large sleek catamaran. They were soon out of the harbour and the giant sails billowed as the wind filled them and the catamaran built up speed. Alfie sat on the front of the boat looking at the beautiful beaches and the lush greenery behind them. The spray from the speeding boats hull kept him cool under the hot sun.

The boats crew were playing all sorts of reggae music and every now and then the Captain would announce some entertainment in the main cabin. Alfie clapped as one of the crew managed to limbo dance underneath two beer bottles with a stick across them. Alfie had a go but he couldn't get any lower than about two feet six inches! That was better than his stiff old Dad who could barely manage four feet!

The time soon passed and the Captain announced that they were about to beach the catamaran on a small island for a barbeque lunch. Alfie, his Dad and Mum had a smashing lunch sat on a rock on the beach. People soon cooled off by swimming in the sea, and sat in little clusters on the beach.

Alfie's dad overheard one man telling the Captain that he had lost his very expensive watch in the water. He offered a $50 reward for anyone who found it, which caused a flurry of activity. All the kids, and a few adults as well, were soon looking up and down the beach and wading into the water.

"Go on, Alfie, have a look," urged his Dad. Alfie paused and thought hard for a moment, then he went on board the boat and borrowed a large clear plastic cake box from the cook. He then walked about in the shallows looking through the bottom of the half submerged cake box. It was perfect for displacing the water so he could see the sandy sea bed clearly.

Soon he had collected a few pretty shells and some small change coins.

He waded out a little deeper and suddenly he saw a flash of light from the bottom. Alfie reached down and could just grasp the item. He shouted as he pulled the watch out. Everyone came running, although some of the children were very disappointed that it wasn't them that found it. The man was so very grateful to get his Rolex watch back that he handed Alfie a crisp new fifty dollar note as reward. Alfie's Dad laughingly said that Alfie could even go on holiday and show a profit!

They sailed on and on around the island; the sea changed to a really dark purple as they went by some high cliffs. The Captain told them that this was due to the water being very deep.

They stopped off in English Harbour for afternoon tea. The Captain told them all about the sugar trade and how the Royal navy used the harbour in the 18th and 19th century as a repair base. He showed them Nelson's Dockyard where Captain Nelson was based until he was promoted to Commander in chief in 1787. The harbour was now filled with expensive yachts bearing flags of many countries on them. The Captain steered the catamaran safely out of the harbour and then sailed back to berth at Jolly Harbour.

Back at the hotel, Alfie's Dad decided to call home to find out how Grampy and Gran were getting on with looking after Eddie. Mum was missing the dog and so was Alfie.

Alfie told Gran about finding the watch in the sea and getting a reward. He was pleased when Gran told him that they had been to Mr Armitage the Butcher's shop and bought Eddie the biggest bone he had. This was a reward for him finding the house keys Grampy had lost in the front garden! Alfie didn't say that he already knew all about it.

The next few days passed quietly with visits to the tourist shops and to an emerald centre where Alfie's Dad bought his Mum a nice ring with a big emerald in it. Alfie played cricket several more times and on the last night, they went to a barbeque on the highest point in Antigua.

"A week is never enough," sighed Mum as the three of them stood watching their last Antiguan sunset. The view as the sun disappeared with the characteristic green flash was spectacular.

The next day was spent packing the cases to go home. Alfie's Dad had to sit on the cases to shut them as they had a lot more to take back than they had arrived with.

They enjoyed a last couple of hours on the beach and then the coach took them back to the airport, where they were soon in the queue checking in.

When they got to the check-in desk they were surprised to see that the man checking them in was the man whose watch Alfie had found. "Hello, young man!" he said cheerily as he tapped away on his screen. "Oh! Look at that! I see that we are able to move you all up to business class, as economy is sadly overbooked." He winked and thanked Alfie again for finding his Rolex.

Alfie's Mum and Dad beamed when they were shown to the Business class seats which were extremely luxurious - and reclined a long way back for added comfort!

It was an overnight flight so the sleeper beds would be most beneficial. After a delicious dinner with some great wines, Alfie's Mum remarked that she would only ever want to fly Business in future! The cabin lights were dimmed; Alfie stretched out and was soonout for the count for the whole night.

Many hours later Alfie woke up to the sound of breakfast being served out. He ate everything that was offered to him and then went to the restroom where he had a wash and brushed his teeth with the "all in one" toothbrush kit from the wash bag the hostess had given him.

The pilot wished them "Good Morning" and told them that they would be landing at Gatwick in about fifteen minutes at 06.30hrs local time. He told them that the weather was unsurprisingly bad! It was raining and it was a cool ten degrees. The passengers all moaned, as it was only yesterday that they were in warm, sunny Antigua, at twenty-five degrees plus!

"Welcome back to England!" the pilot joked.

Alfie was soon off the plane and had collected the family luggage on a big trolley. He was going through the customs hall when he saw a sniffer dog checking the bags as people walked by. "Eddie could do that if they were looking for bones!" he said to his Dad.

Dad tooted the car horn as they pulled up in front of their house. Grampy opened the front door and Eddie came bounding out to meet Alfie. He knocked him over as he jumped up and licked his face, his hands, his neck and his nose. Alfie dashed in and unpacked his case. He carefully took out the two presents that he had secretively bought on holiday using his $50 reward.

His Grampy and Gran were pleased when he gave them one of the pictures of the boys playing cricket. His Mum was even more pleased when he gave her the second one. "If you look carefully," he said, "you can see me fielding in the back, with my feet in the sea!"

Chapter Three
Joust In Time!

Alfie spent the rest of the day telling Grampy and Gran all about the holiday. He also made a big fuss of Eddie and gave him a good brushing. Eddies coat was shining like black glass when he finished.

After tea Grampy decided to play football in the garden with Alfie and Eddie. He lasted about five minutes before he sat on the garden bench puffed out. Eddie was keeping goal as Alfie tried to put the ball past him. Eddie was too good at it and Alfie only managed to score two goals all evening.

Soon it was bedtime and Alfie and Eddie went to bed. The sheets on the bed covered Alfie in a huge white envelope and he could hear a voice saying "Come and rest little man, you have had a busy, busy, day."

The trumpets sounded, the people cheered as Lord Alfred de Moreteyne (commonly known as Lord Alfie) rode into the tournament arena. He was covered in shiny steel armour. His squire had been up all night polishing it ready for the tournament. The Shire horse he rode was snorting hot misty breath from its nostrils. It always got excited at the prospect of jousting, which is a medieval form of sporting warfare using lances that shatter on impact and are not usually lethal!

All around the field the people fell silent as the King and Queen of England took their places and the announcements were made. The challenge was issued and the knights assembled in a line. They tipped their lances to salute the Royals before the draw was announced. Lord Alfred drew Sir Roland of Beaumont for his first opponent. A fair sort of chap, thought Alfie, but still a strong opponent.

The two knights faced each other at opposite ends of the arena. They lowered their visors and with a tilt of their lances, they spurred their steeds towards each other. They each crouched down aiming the lance at their opponents' body as they thundered at each other. Crash! They each hit each other on their shields and shattered their soft-ended lances. Both men stayed on their horses, though Sir Roland rocked back in his saddle.

"One hit each!" announced the official.

William the squire hastily gave Lord Alfred another lance. The contestants turned and raced at each other again. Alfie leaned all his weight behind the lance and struck Sir Roland full in the chest and unhorsed him. Sir Roland fell flat on his back and was winded. Lord Alfred had won this match. Who would he face in the next round? He noticed that the beautiful Lady Grace was in the crowd watching; as he passed by she waved to him.

Lord Alfred was given a bye into the final as both of the knights in the earlier round had retired after hurting each other badly. He was just preparing for the next round when he heard the crowds booing, he sent his squire William out to find out what was going on. He came back two minutes later and said that Baron Ernst De Blacque had just beaten his opponent, the Lord of Worcester, with a questionable blow from his sword. Lord had been struck with a lance, unhorsed and was now very dazed. The Baron was not a popular contender because nobody likes a cheat.

It was the final and Lord Alfred was now facing Baron Ernst de Blacque. They glared at each other through their visors, dipped their lances, urged on their horses and rode at each other with grim determination. The two lances shattered into matchsticks and the crowd gasped as both knights managed to stay mounted.

The crowd cheered on Lord Alfred and booed Baron De Blacque. The Baron suddenly asked for a short break as his horse had lost a shoe. The Field Marshall examined it and found the shoe to be missing, so he ordered a ten-minute break for the blacksmith to put a new shoe on.

Lord Alfred took a break as well and went and sat in his tent until he was called back. Whilst he was away, William the squire checked Lord Alfred's horse, checking the reins, the saddle and making sure that the girth strap was tight enough. He had been distracted for only a minute, but it was time enough for Baron de Blacque's squire to creep up and weaken the girth strap with a small cut from his knife.

The tournament final restarted. The two knights were charging at each other when Lord Alfred felt his saddle start to slip very slightly. He pressed home his attack and slipped slightly to the left. This made the Baron miss his target, but he made contact in full with his lance and he unseated the Baron who fell with a crash. He had won three points to one.

Lord Alfred just managed to dismount as the heavy saddle slipped under his horse and fell off under the strain. Lord Alfred looked at the girth and saw that it had been cut. He had been lucky this time but he felt that he would meet the Baron Ernst De Blacque again! And next time he would know to watch him very carefully. The man was an unremitting cheat!

The King presented the Champion with a miniature silver lance as his prize; the crowd cheered and the Lady Grace was smiling and clapping at her heroic Lord Alfred's victory. The evil Baron De Blacque stormed off in a temper at losing. Not just a cheat, but also a very poor loser!

A banquet was arranged for that evening and the champion and his lady were invited to attend and sit next to the King. Alone up in her room, Lady Grace was just about to leave her apartments in the castle to go to the banquet, when Baron de Blacque and his squire burst in and put a big sack over her head. She tried to scream and fight; in the struggle Lady Grace

dropped a silk headscarf; a small table was knocked over and the water jug spilt. They carried her off into the night! As they galloped out of the castle they knocked over several guards who were trying to stop them. The alarm was raised! The Lady Grace had been kidnapped by Baron de Blacque.

William the squire dashed in to tell Lord Alfred, who shot out of bed and threw on some clothes. He called to his faithful hound, Eddie, and they all dashed to Lady Grace's room to find only the mess caused by the struggle. Lord Alfred picked up the scarf and got Eddie to sniff it before putting it in his pocket.

"Come on boy! Seek!" he urged. Eddie was soon leading them down the steps, across the yard and out over the moat into the trees. They tracked the scent for many hours and had covered about three miles when they saw a small campfire in the distance.

Lord Alfred crept up to the campsite where he saw three men, including Baron De Blacque. Behind them was a rough tent where he could just make out the elegant form of Lady Grace through the open entrance... she was tied up to the centre pole. He heard the Baron tell his squire to mount a guard on the tent.

Lord Alfred could see that a frontal attack would lead to a fight and harm could come to the Lady Grace. Using the trees for cover Lord Alfred crept back to Eddie and his squire. They retreated a short way and Lord Alfred whispered instructions to his squire.

About an hour later, a knight approached the camp in brightly polished armour on a shire horse and carrying the shield of Lord Alfred of Moreteyne. He stopped a hundred yards away.

The knight beat his sword on his shield to get Baron De Blacque's attention. He gave the Baron fifteen minutes to prepare to defend himself to the death. The Baron called for his squire to help him put his armour on, shouting that he was going to sort out Lord Alfred once and for all - as he believed the knight to be Lord Alfred. The Baron's squire dashed round helping his master to get ready.

Whilst this frantic preparation was going on, a knife was splitting open the back of the tent. Lady Grace heard the sound and turned her head, frightened at the frenzy of activity happening around her. She gasped as she saw Lord Alfred so he quickly put his finger to his lips to tell her to keep quiet. Working rapidly, Lord Alfred had soon cut the ropes that held Lady Grace and they sneaked silently out of the back of the tent. He told her to hide in the trees with Eddie.

Lord Alfred then crept up alongside the Baron's horse, well hidden by the darkness, and carefully cut the girth strap nearly through. The terrified squire was too busy watching the fearsome knight a hundred yards away. The Baron strode up, mounted his horse, waved his sword and spurred his horse towards the knight he believed to be Lord Alfred. He got about twenty yards, and had just built up a bit of speed, when his girth strap snapped completely and he fell very heavily, knocking himself out.

Lord Alfred and his trusty squire William stepped out of the shadows and tied up the Baron and his men, using the same rope that had tied up the Lady Grace!

The Baron soon came round and was cursing how stupid he had been allowing himself to be tricked by the cunning Lord Alfred. They marched back to the castle just as dawn was breaking. The lady Grace was so grateful to Lord Alfred of Moreteyne that she kissed him.

A big wet licking sort of kiss woke Alfie up! It was Eddie asking to be let out into the garden! Before slipping out of bed to open the door for Eddie, Alfie felt under his pillow and he found a beautiful miniature silver lance. He carefully wrapped it in a Kleenex tissue and stowed it away in his treasure drawer.

Chapter Four
Well Oill Be...

Grampy and Gran were all ready to go home. Alfie's Dad had packed their cases into the back of Grampy's Trusty old MGB GT V8 sports car – as Grampy might be old but he still enjoyed his speedy little sportscar. Alfie felt a little tearful as he hugged them goodbye and Eddie woofed sadly as they got into the car and waved goodbye. Grampy tooted the horn and roared off down the street.

Alfie's Dad said that Grampy ought to behave like a pensioner and not like he was eighteen! Mum said that she wished she could have Grampy and Gran's energy when she was their age!

Alfie had just sat down to read his comic in the lounge when the doorbell rang.

It was his best friends, William and Grace. They knew he was back from holiday and had come to see if he wanted to play in the Park across the road. Eddie jumped around excitedly, knowing exactly what was going on. Alfie grabbed his small backpack, raided the fridge for goodies and ran out the front door - barely before his mum could say "Bye! Have a nice time!"

The three friends walked and chatted about Alfie's holiday, whilst Eddie ran to and fro, sniffing here and there. They then told him what had gone on while he had been away. Grace and William wanted to show Alfie a new tree house they had been building in the woods at the back of the park. Alfie was really impressed when he saw the huge old tree and the platform that William and Grace had built in it. "We got all the old planks from the collapsed shed in William's garden, and his dad lent us some tools to make the planks fit," explained Grace.

Alfie climbed up the rope leading to the platform and the other two joined him. They could see for quite a long distance from that height - in fact, from one side of the park to the other.

Alfie shared his goodies with them and they talked about putting a roof over the platform. Alfie knew that his dad had got an old tarpaulin in his garage; perhaps he would let them have it. They ran back home and Mr Nelson agreed to let them use it. After lunch, later that afternoon, the friends heaved the green tarpaulin up the tree and secured the corners of it on the boughs above. "Perfect!" said Alfie. "It makes for good camouflage."

The three friends descended the rope to the park, deciding to play football. They used their jumpers as goal posts and all took it in turns to try to score penalty shots. After about an hour they decided to return to the tree house.

They were shocked to find that Butch Grimsdale (the school bully) and his mates were up on the platform and had pulled the rope up. "Clear off you wallies! It's our tree house now!" said Butch, lobbing a flour bomb in Alfie's direction. It burst on the grass beside him; a cloud of fine white flour welled up and made the three friends cough and retreat. "Run away to Mummy!" taunted Butch, as his two mates Eric and Murdoch laughed and waved at them.

Alfie, William and Grace decided to call it a night and went to walk home. They decided to sleep on the problem and work out how to get the tree house back and keep it! Alfie knew that they would have to outsmart Butch and his mates, as they were a lot bigger than him and William – but had much smaller brains too!

Alfie went to bed that night thinking about the tree house and how to get it back.

Eddie was in his basket beside the bed, he was flat on his back with his feet in the air. He was doing an impression worthy of a small steam train as he snored. Alfie pulled the pillows over his head and yawned.

The train stopped with a whistle and a screech as it braked to a halt in the small dusty station in Northern Delhi in the north part of India. The station was a hubbub of people who were either travelling or had come to beg from people wealthy enough to travel. Alfie had travelled to the north of Delhi in order to survey the land for oil, at the invitation of the Sultan who had asked for the Best Man for the Job. Alfie the surveyor stood waiting, surrounded by poor street children who clamoured round him, offering to show him around the city for a few rupees.

Alfie was soon out of small coins when a large, grand Indian gentleman in a turban with a large ruby in the centre, shooed them away.

"Mr Alfie, I presume?" said the gentleman who introduced himself as The Sultan of Amritsar - the region of India about two hundered and fifty miles north of Delhi. This was the man that Alfie the surveyor was there to meet. The Sultan's man carried all of Alfie's bags to an ancient Rolls Royce and loaded them on the back, whilst the Sultan's other men were loading the scientific boxes into a large van nearby. Alfie took his place in the car with the Sultan and they were off at a leisurely pace toward the Sultan's Palace.

The Sultan showed Alfie the Golden temple of Amritsar and explained that it is the most holy shrine of the Sikhs. Amritsar was once the capital of the Punjab (The Land of Five Rivers), and the Sultan explained that the Dalai Lama lived there now, in exile after the Chinese took over Tibet. The Sultan said he would introduce him to Alfie, which Alfie realised was a big honour.

Alfie was shown to a lavish guest room where he washed

and cooled off after his long train trip from Bombay via Delhi. Tea was served at three o'clock and the Sultan discussed with Alfie the possibility of oil being found in the foothills. Alfie explained that if there was any oil, he would find it with his latest equipment.

The Sultan said, "Alfie would be granted any favour he requests if he finds oil in the Sultan's region."

The next day, Alfie the surveyor had his computer navigation system checked and he unloaded all the strings of ground sensors and thoroughly checked them over. His investigations of satellite maps had shown him the best geological features where oil might be found. He set off for the foothills in a white four-wheel drive with his driver who was also a local guide and an explosives expert.

Alfie the surveyor laid out the sensors in ten long straight lines and connected them up to his laptop. When all was ready he asked the driver to set off a small charge in the ground. The sound-wave from the explosion travelled down into the earth and bounced back off the rock formations. The sensors picked up the returning waves and, on the laptop, plotted a map of the underlying rock strata (which are layers of rock).

Alfie the surveyor and the driver spent all day going along the foothills setting off charges and taking readings. Finally, the driver pitched camp and they ate a chicken curry. Alfie the surveyor had just plugged his laptop into the car to charge, when his stomach started gurgling and he felt that he needed the toilet in a hurry! He dashed off to the toilet tent and remained there most of the night - much to the amusement of the driver. In the morning Alfie the surveyor was feeling better after the driver had given him a local cure for what he called "Delhi Belly".

They were just surveying the last section when Alfie noticed some tar on the driver's boots. Tar comes from oil deposits! He asked the driver where he had just walked and he laid out the sensors in that area. The charge was set off and the readings came back to Alfie the surveyor's laptop.

"Success!" shouted Alfie the surveyor, as a large domed shape full of oil showed up on the screen. Alfie pressed a button and took a satellite fix on the area, ready to now return back to the Palace with the good news.

The Sultan was very pleased indeed! This meant that his country would be richer as they were now self sufficient in oil; it meant that the Sultan, as the ruler of his region, could help the poor people.

The Sultan took Alfie the surveyor to meet the Dalai Lama, as he had promised, and asked him to bless Alfie, as this was the man who brought wealth to the Sultanate. The Dalai Lama looked at Alfie and thanked and blessed him, as the country needed the wealth to help the many poor in the region.

Alfie had never met a man who looked as calm and wise. He gave Alfie the surveyor a painting of The Wheel of Life. He said that it showed the various stages of the life of man and how he must move from one stage to another by doing good deeds and becoming a better person until he became fully enlightened. That afternoon Alfie the surveyor studied the painting and wondered which stage he was at in the wheels picture. It was only after a very grand dinner given in his honour by the Sultan that he realized what he must do.

The Sultan asked him to name his reward for finding the oil. He remembered the street children at the station and he asked that a school be set up at the railway side to help feed, clothe and educate the street children. The Sultan was so pleased at Alfie's very unselfish idea that he decided that a school would be set up at every railway station. All the people at the dinner stood and applauded the idea and the Dalai Lama smiled at Alfie; it was like a burst of bright sunlight hitting him in the face.

"Get up, lazybones!" called his Mother as she opened the curtains wide and let the sun shine in. Alfie reached under his pillow and found a beautiful picture of The Wheel of Life.

Chapter Five
Above One's Station

A brilliant idea had occurred to Alfie since his dream last night. The other morning, he had seen his father munching on a few squares of chocolate, followed by a small glass of syrup. Alfie had asked for some, but his father had laughed and said that it was a type of laxative, designed to help you go to the toilet. Alfie had turned up his nose and decided he didn't want any after all. Going to the toilet merely interrupted valuable playing time!

After dressing himself quickly, he nipped downstairs and removed two jars from the pantry shelf.

"Just taking Eddie to the park, mum!" he called, hiding the jars in his jacket. He and Eddie ran to the tree house. It was still early morning as Alfie climbed the tree house and left his backpack on the platform.

Alfie then took Eddie for the rest of his walk and went home to breakfast. He sat eating his breakfast with a smile on his face from ear to ear! "Okay!" said his Dad. "What are you up to now?"

"Oh nothing much, Dad," said Alfie, and asked if he could phone William and Grace up to arrange to meet them in the park. He told them to meet him at the tree house as he had a plan to get one over on Butch and his dim mates. He also briefed his two pals on what to say and when.

Soon they were up on the platform and on lookout. Sure enough, at about ten o'clock Butch, Eric and Murdoch came into view. As they came nearer they saw Alfie, William and Grace up in the tree. They shouted in surprise when they spotted

Alfie and his pals scrambling down from the platform and making off in the other direction.

Butch and his gang had already climbed up the tree, when they overheard Grace telling Alfie that he had left his rucksack with the sweets and cola on the platform.

Butch seized the rucksack and emptied the contents of bars of chocolate and a bottle of cola onto the platform. He threw the empty rucksack back on the floor to Alfie and said that he, Eric and Murdoch were going to scoff all of his chocolate and drink his Cola. Alfie, William and Grace all shouted in dismay.

"It's ours!" William called up. "Give it back to us, and we can all share it."

"No! We're going to eat and drink it all!" Butch crowed, and the greedy boys promptly ate all the chocolate and drunk the cola. Alfie, William and Grace looked all glum as the chocolate wrappers and the empty cola bottle were tossed to the ground.

The three friends sat and waited for about twenty minutes pretended to be really disappointed but secretly sharing little smiles. Finally Alfie asked Butch if he was feeling all right.

Butch was just about to tell him to clear off, when he felt his stomach start to bubble and rumble as if it was going to explode. Eric and Murdoch suddenly felt the same. They all started to dash down the rope and run across the park to the toilets. Unfortunately they were still locked, as the Park keeper had not opened them up yet. The three were last seen running as fast as they could back home. Alfie and his two pals laughed their heads off!

Alfie had decided not to get mad, but to get even with them. He had taken laxative chocolate and syrup of figs from the pantry, which he had added to the cola!

"Round one to us!" said Alfie, as they all high-fived each other. William and Grace thought that it would be a while before Butch and his mates tried to take the tree house over again.

Eddie was waiting in the front garden when Alfie got back. He was very excited to see him and he jumped up and tried to lick Alfie's face. "To see him act like that, anyone would think that you had been away in outer space for a month!" said his Mum.

Alfie's Mum had made tea and set it out on a table in the garden as the day had warmed up nicely. They had Eddie's favourite which was strawberries and cream - only Eddie liked it without the strawberries! Alfie and Eddie played in the garden until it was dark, then came in to sit in the lounge watching television until his Dad sent him up to bed because he couldn't keep his eyes open. Alfie lay on the bed, closed his eyes and started to sink into the softness of the mattress.

*

10. 9. 8. 7. 6. 5. 4. 3. 2. 1. Ignition and Blastoff! The Challenger spacecraft lifted off from the Cape. Vast clouds of white smoke came from the base of the giant rockets as the Challenger streaked skywards. Commander Alfie and his crew were pressed down on their seats as the forces of gravity were fighting the ships ascent. Soon they reached over seventeen thousand miles an hour and the Earth's atmosphere got thinner and thinner as the Sun reflected brightly off the edge of it.

The pressure eased and Commander Alfie watched the booster rockets fall away and drop back to Earth. The crew, made up of Astronauts William and Grace, were busy talking to ground control. They were checking the navigation screen and locking in a course for the orbiting space station.

They all took off their helmets and marvelled as they floated weightlessly around the cabin; until they were stowed away Commander Alfie guided the Challenger into the docking lock on the space station. Whirr, Click, Thunk, the docking was successful. The airlock was opened and the two-man crew on the station welcomed Commander Alfie and his crew on board.

The next hour was a hive of activity as the stores and equipment were offloaded on to the space station. Gallons of oxygen and water were transferred as it all had to last the station for the next four months.

After a break for dinner, the work on the special experiment was to begin. Commander Alfie put on his full helmet and suit and prepared for a space walk to install the special aerials and dish on the outside of the station. He strapped himself into the small rocket pack and the Challengers cargo doors opened. He eased himself gently out of the bay, into the bright sunlight and with a few short rocket bursts was alongside the station. He hitched the safety strap to the station and started work on the Aerial and dish installation.

He finished the installation and connected it all up. Then just as he disconnected his safety strap, he was hit in the battery pack by a very small high-speed space particle, which knocked out his electric controls. He started to drift very slowly away from the station and the Challenger. Trying not panic but instead thinking clearly and quickly, he realized that the new experiment could save him. His radio was still working on back up but the signal was very weak. He radioed Astronaut Grace to track him and he outlined his plan.

He reached in his small toolbox and by undoing one of his pack straps he could reach the damaged panel. Working quickly he unscrewed the panel and pulled out the two wires from the disabled battery. He had some silver duct tape in his toolbox and he taped each wire separately to the outside of the rocket packs plastic exterior. Each wire was marked by a big conductive X of duct tape.

He strapped himself back into the rocket pack and he told Grace that he was ready.

Astronaut Grace targeted the two X's with two small laser beams from the station's new aerials. The beams were locked on by computer and the stations nuclear generator was

connected to them. Astronaut Grace held her breath as she pressed the button.

The electricity travelled down the beams in the vacuum of space and hit the X's. Commander Alfie's controls suddenly lit up and he was able to back towards the Challenger's open bay, using the power from the laser beam electricity. The experiment proved a successful idea and Commander Alfie was saved! The laser beams could provide power to spaceships over vast distances from the space station so that their weight and size could be lessened by not needing so much fuel or batteries.

Commander Alfie was lucky to be alive! It was with a huge sense of relief that he was soon on his way back to Earth. He put the Challenger into reverse aspect to slow it down in orbit and eased the nose into position for re-entry. The glow from the heat shield got redder and redder from the friction of the thickening atmosphere. Commander Alfie eased back the controls and the Challenger slowed until the landing strip came into view. Escorted by two fighter planes, the wheels touched down and a braking parachute was deployed to slow the Challenger. The craft came to a halt and was soon surrounded by helicopters and vehicles of all kinds.

Commander Alfie and his crew stepped from the Challenger and a band struck up the National Anthem. The President was there to present the crew with a medal each to celebrate their achievement and safe return. Commander Alfie proudly saluted as the medal was pinned on his uniform.

The pin stuck in his chest. Alfie woke up, with a claw from Eddie digging into his chest; the dog was trying to tell him that his radio alarm clock had just gone off! Alfie looked under his pillow and found a large uniform badge embroidered with "Commander Alfie Nelson, NASA Challenger Mission 18".

Chapter Six
A Shot at Dawn

Later that day, Alfie, William and Grace were all chatting at break time over a glass of milk. They were discussing the victory over Butch, Eric and Murdoch at the tree house when the bully-boys arrived for their break. Alfie and all the other classmates held up a piece of toilet paper and asked Butch and his mates if they needed to be excused! The class all burst into laughter and Butch went bright red and stormed out of the classroom.

That afternoon in geography class they were learning all about the moon and its effect on the tides. The teacher told them that in some places the tide went up and down by thirty feet; this meant that when the tide flowed in it could be as fast as a man galloping a horse. He said that this was particularly the case at Mont St Michel just off the coast of France. As the bell rang for the end of school, the teacher handed them all some homework to do which was to learn all about Mont St Michel, and to give their opinion as to why the tide fluctuated so much.

When he got home, Alfie got his atlas out and began to draw a copy of the coastline at Mont St Michel. He then drew an outline of the low water mark and was amazed to find it was over a mile from the high tide mark. He drew in the Channel Islands and then marked in the French towns of St Malo, Cancale and Avranches.

Alfie tucked the map away in his satchel for school the next day and joined his Dad to watch television before bed. His Dad loved old films, particularly period war films with secret agents. Alfie watched the film about Captain Hornblower until his eyelids were drooping. Dad sent him to bed and he very soon nodded off to sleep.

The deck of *The Labrador* was busy with sailors scrubbing and polishing the decks. Sailors were up the mast adjusting the sails and rigging. They were on their way home to Portsmouth after a long time fighting the French fleet, and Captain Alfie had decided to return back home to port to stock up his very depleted store of food, gunpowder and shot. They had just passed Land's End when a signal rocket flew up from the look-out station on the shore. A man was standing up on the highest coastal point with two flags and started to signal to *The Labrador.* First Officer William noted the long message down and gave it to Captain Alfie.

It read:

Proceed immediately to Avranches and meet our agent (Codename Bulldog) and return. Do not get detected, mission most secret! Use your discretion if necessary.

Captain Alfie's men were none too pleased not to be going home but they set to and soon *The Labrador* was sailing under cover of darkness - with no lights at all - to a point just off Avranches. A small rowing boat approached the ship and after the code "Bulldog" was exchanged, a tough looking man was helped on to the deck. Captain Alfie ordered full sail and *The Labrador* sailed into the night.

Bulldog the spy (who looked like Butch Grimsdale) was soon in the Captain's cabin.

He told Captain Alfie that the French Fleet was moored in Avranches harbour and that they were going out to sea to attack the main British fleet on the next evening tide. By the time they got back to England with the news it would be too late. He asked Captain Alfie if there was any way that *The Labrador* could mount an attack and catch the fleet when it was bottled up in the harbour.

Captain Alfie said that he would like to attack the French but his stocks were very low and that he was going to restock his ship when he was diverted to meet "Bulldog".

However he had studied the charts and the tide tables and he believed that, with Bulldog's information on the French defences, he had a plan… which might just work.

Captain Alfie ordered *The Labrador* to be turned round and asked for the officers to join him in his cabin to brief them on his plan.

A short while later, a small boat containing Captain Alfie, Bulldog and several tough sailors, left the side of *The Labrador* in the dark and rowed to a small inlet near Avranches. The moored up silently and climbed directly up a cliff path, coming up on the guards and catching them completely unawares. Within minutes they had overpowered the guards of a cliff top battery that Bulldog had told them about. They tied the Frenchmen up and stole their uniforms.

Captain Alfie and his men then put on the stolen uniforms; the only one to fit Captain Alfie properly was that of a private. They then loaded a large horse cart up with gunpowder and set off around Avranches until they were a short way upstream of the river, which flowed into and through the Harbour at low tide.

The Harbour was protected from a seaward attack by a large boom of small barges and chains, some half a mile out to sea. 'This might have kept the British out but it also kept the French in,' thought Captain Alfie, planning his next attack.

Captain Alfie and his men soon found an unoccupied barge moored by the riverside. They were just loading the gunpowder on board when a guard asked them what they were up to at that time of the morning. Captain Alfie explained in perfect French that the French Commander wanted extra gunpowder on board his ships for the fight with the English. The guard accepted his story and walked off a short distance and leant against a wall to watch the boat being loaded.

The tide was turning and the level in the harbour was dropping just as it became light. The guard might not have been that clever, but he suddenly realized that all the sailors were in artillery outfits and they were taking their orders from a lowly private. He lowered his musket and marched towards the boat party. He ordered them to put their hands up and explain what they were doing. He didn't see the large figure of Bulldog creep up behind him and crack him on the head. The guard fell in a heap, but as he did so, his musket fired.

Captain Alfie and his men lit a slow fuse and let the large wooden barge drift down stream towards the Harbour. Captain Alfie jumped on to the cart and with his men hidden under a tarpaulin in the back, he set off quickly along the road towards Mont St Michel.

Guards were running in all directions to see who had raised the alarm by firing that single shot. Captain Alfie looked back over his shoulder to see the barge explode and catch fire. The French ships captains were all of a panic as the fire ship drifted towards their ships. Their ships were stuck on the bottom and couldn't move as the flat-bottomed barge drifted towards them in the river's current.

The barge collided with a battleship which caught fire and exploded, showering flames over some of the other closely moored French fleet. That's scuppered them! Captain Alfie thought, as he made his way along the now dry seabed road to Mont St Michel.

As they approached the island fortress, a guard challenged them. This time Bulldog, who was wearing the Artillery Sergeant's uniform, said in French that they were the relief party sent to take over the small gun battery on the Mont. The garrison of six men were pleased to be told that they could take three days leave; they didn't argue but instead they just left as fast as they could towards the ale houses of Avranches.

Captain Alfie and his crew soon made the Mont's few cannons unusable by hammering spikes in the fuse holes of the guns. They then followed the outgoing tide out into the English Channel.

They had not gone very far when the French garrison realised that they had been duped and that ships were on fire in the Harbour. Indeed the explosions and smoke could quite plainly be heard *and* seen. The French were in hot pursuit across the sands when Captain Alfie and his crew reached the low water mark. There, a few yards out to sea, was a waiting longboat and crew from *The Labrador* under First Officer William.

Captain Alfie and the shore crew were glad to see the boat and they hoped that the plan would work. They dragged themselves through the tide, which was just on the turn and were helped into the boat. The French were still chasing them and were just in firing range when they found that the water was starting to get deeper all of a sudden. In blind panic, they threw their muskets, swords and powder away and tried to outrun the incoming tide. They were soon swamped and they were heard cursing the English saboteurs as they swam back towards the shore.

Captain Alfie and all the crew were soon safely back on *The Labrador*. Even though the ship was in range of the Mont's guns, they had been spiked and couldn't be used.

The crew celebrated the raid with a huge dinner of all the rations left on ship, with a background of fires from the French Fleet which could be seen over twenty miles away.

Captain Alfie and Bulldog had saved a lot of British lives and the only shot fired had been by a French guard by accident! The crew called for three cheers.

"I said! Wake up cloth-ears!" said Mum, who had been calling up the stairs for Alfie to get up for five minutes. Alfie wiped the sleep from his eyes and felt under his pillow. He found a small spike like the ones Captain Alfie hammered into the gun fuse holes on Mont St Michel.

Chapter Seven
A Trip Down Under

Today was Saturday and it was Mrs Nelson's day to help out at the Beach Café in Sandcastle Bay. As usual, on a nice day she took Alfie and Eddie with her.

Alfie stocked up the picnic benches with salt and pepper pots and put up the big umbrellas.

Grace's Dad, Angus Anthony, owned the café and he was busy cooking bacon and eggs for the customers. Grace said "Hi "as she sat beside Eddie and gave him half of her sausage sandwich. Eddie licked his lips as the brown sauce on it was a bit spicy for him, but he still managed to eat his share! After breakfast, Alfie and Grace played nearby on the sand and were soon digging in the sand, making sandcastles.

Alfie was kidding Eddie that he had buried a bone in the sand. "Seek boy! Just here! Good dog!" Eddie was digging madly with his front paws and a spray of sand was flying up behind him. Eddie's claws made a grating noise, which made Alfie and Grace peer into the huge hole that he had dug. There at the bottom of it was a domed object with a bright yellow scratch in the top from Eddie's claws.

Alfie and Grace jumped into the pit and started to scrape away the sand from the object. It was like a sort of metal crash helmet with a round glass screen on the front and a piece of pipe out the back. It was very heavy and Alfie needed Grace to help lift it out onto the beach. Alfie soon realised that it was an old fashion brass diving helmet. He scraped the heavy wet sand out of it and carried it into the beach café to show Grace's Dad and his Mum.

"That looks an old beauty," said Angus. "I heard that there used to be a diving and salvage yard in the bay, but that was years ago."

Alfie and Grace spent the rest of the day cleaning and playing with the helmet, whilst Eddie went chasing rabbits on the sand dunes. That night, Alfie proudly showed his dad the helmet when he got home. His Dad offered to give it a good clean in the shed with his power polisher. Alfie watched as the dark helmet turned to a polished golden brass colour. He could see his face reflected in it; although it made him look very fat faced because the helmet had a rounded surface.

Alfie's Dad suggested that as he had a spare light fitting and he could fix it inside the helmet to make it into a bedside lamp, which Alfie thought was a fantastic idea. He looked up at his Dad admiringly – he was so inventive!

That night Alfie looked at the illuminated helmet and the shadows it threw over his bedroom as he lay in bed. He closed his eyes and he wondered how it would feel to be a deep-sea diver and also who had worn the helmet.

A large conger eel flicked his tail as it swam past, outside of the small window that Alfie the deep-sea diver was looking through. He was being lowered to the ocean floor in a metal platform cage. The cage settled on the sand and Alfie the deep-sea diver unlocked the side and stepped out.

Each step he took was hard work as he had a big heavy set of lead boots on. The air was being pumped down to him from the ship above and it came in gushes down a long thin pipe.

He was searching for a lost ship, which had sunk with a valuable cargo of gold bars. The bars were being sent to the American colonies to pay the troops guarding them, and the administrators running them.

The ship, called *The Empress of India,* had been caught in a storm at night and had hit a reef and sunk. Several of the crew had survived the sinking and had made it to a nearby island. In the dark and storm they lost their bearings and could only write down roughly where they thought *The Empress of India* had gone down. Alfie the Diver was following up a sighting of a large dark shape in the water, seen by the spotter in a helium balloon that was tethered to the mast of the diving ship. He checked his wrist compass and walked toward the sighting area. He soon found a cannon barrel half sticking out of the sandy bottom.

The signs were looking good! He saw another cannon barrel a short way ahead. He kept striding in the direction of the second barrel and he soon found himself standing on the edge of a large deep-sea ravine. The water was so deep that he couldn't see the bottom. He strained his eyes to look into the abyss.

Then about fifty feet below him he saw the ship. It was *The Empress of India*! She was wedged between two outcrops of rock but otherwise appeared to be remarkably intact. Alfie the diver tugged his safety rope and gave a signal that he wanted to be brought up to the surface. The platform was soon beside him and he got in it.

He went up in stages to avoid getting "the bends". Divers can suffer very badly from dissolved gas in the blood which expands as they come up from a dive, as the water pressure gets less nearer the surface. They have to go slowly and allow the body to re-adjust to the changing pressure.

Alfie the Diver was soon on the ship's deck explaining the situation to his crew. It would need to be a two-man job for him and Angus, the other diver, and it would be very dangerous, as The Empress was stuck between two rock outcrops and could tip over into the abyss.

The next day as the sun was coming up over the Caribbean, Alfie the Diver went down to the wreck. He noticed a hole in the ships side that exposed the cargo hold. He cautiously stepped inside and saw that the gold bullion boxes were still intact although they were all piled up on one side. He wrapped a thin steel cable around two boxes and hooked them up to the winch cable from the ship. With a pull on his signal rope, the winch cable tightened and the two boxes were hoisted up to the diving ship.

Alfie the Diver worked for about another twenty minutes and sent up another two boxes. It was then time to go back up himself and let the other diver take over.

Angus was working away as Alfie the Diver took a breather on the deck. More gold boxes came up and soon it was time for Alfie the Diver to go back down again.

He had just had his face glass screwed on tightly when he noticed the rest of the crew looking in horror at the frayed and broken safety rope from Angus, the other diver. They were still pumping air down so he must still be connected to the airline.

Alfie the Diver went straight down to the bottom to find that Angus was wrapped in large green tentacles from a huge octopus that had come from its lair in the back section of the ship – and Angus did not appear to be conscious! As Alfie swam towards him, he was suddenly gripped by a flailing tentacle, which dragged him towards the giant sized parrot shaped beak of the octopus. The beak opened and closed threateningly. He was being squeezed so tightly and he felt himself start to black out. He fought it as he drew his diving knife.

Alfie swiftly stabbed his knife into the tentacle and twisted it. The huge octopus was so shocked that it shot out a cloudy squirt of black ink and let go of the two divers. Alfie the Diver grabbed his unconscious friend and tugged the line on the cage to be lifted up.

The cage was very heavy with the two men and the last remaining box of gold. The winch lifted them up slowly, pausing every now and then for them to avoid the bends.

Angus came around and gestured his thanks to Alfie the Diver.

Suddenly a large green tentacle wrapped around Angus again. The octopus had come back!

Alfie the Diver quickly cut a length of rope from Angus's broken safety line and tied one end tightly to the octopus tentacle. The platform cage was spinning wildly and Alfie the Diver fought hard to keep in it, as he tied the other end of the rope to the heavy gold bullion box. Angus fought the giant octopus, as Alfie the diver needed all his strength to heave the gold box over the side of the platform. The heavy gold box plummeted straight down to the depths and took the octopus on the rope with it. The box hit *The Empress of India* on the front of its bows and, with a grinding of timbers, the ship, octopus and last box of gold went down and down into the abyss until they were out of sight.

The cage and two divers hit the side of the ship as they were hoisted up clear of the water and into the bright sunlight.

Alfie woke up with a start to find Eddie had jumped on the bed and slumped down beside him. The sun was lighting up the curtains just as the alarm went off. Alfie reached under his pillow and found a short length of cut diving rope with a frayed end and a host of tiny barnacle shells on it. He examined it closely before opening the drawer under his bed and carefully put the rope away with his other treasures.

Chapter Eight
Jump On The Green

It was Sunday and after breakfast Alfie went to the park with Eddie. He was walking along with Eddie on his lead when they came to a park bench with an old chap sitting on it.

"Hello boy," said the old man to Eddie and he leaned forward to stroke him on the head. Eddie stopped and let the old man stroke his head; he especially liked it when his ears were stroked. "And what's your name?" asked the man, looking at Eddie's nametag.

"His name's Eddie," supplied Alfie.

The old man introduced himself as Jimmy and Alfie said that he knew his face – wasn't he the milkman? Jimmy said yes, but he had recently retired. He told Alfie that he once knew all the people in the area by first name and how much he now missed the early morning deliveries to everyone's doorstep. He said it was nice then to know that people relied on him. He said the only other time that he had felt like that was when he was a Sergeant in the Second World War.

Alfie asked him, "What happened? Did you shoot anyone?"

He said that he had been in a parachute regiment and that he had fought in France on and after "D Day". He said that a dog like Eddie had once saved his unit. He told Alfie of the hardships and the friends that he had lost in the fighting. He said that the only way to survive had been to be bold and to stick together.

"Not boring you, Alfie, am I?" asked Jimmy, peering sideways at Alfie who had sat down on the bench beside him.

"Oh no, I am quite enjoying it!"

"Mmm. But war's not enjoyable," said Jimmy. "It should always be the last thing that you want to do."

Just then the church bell started ringing and Jimmy got up to go to the morning service. "See you again, young man," said Jimmy as he tottered off.

Alfie and Eddie walked round the park a bit longer before returning home to Acacia drive. The smell of roast beef coming from the kitchen was totally delicious, and Eddie decided to sit by the oven and guard it.

"Just in case it tries to get away!" laughed Alfie.

"Or that we all eat it whilst his back is turned," agreed his mother with a smile.

Alfie set the table with the cutlery. He then put out water glasses and the salt and pepper pots. His Mother came in from the garden with an armful of freshly cut flowers and Alfie opened the door for her. "Thank you! My proper little gentleman!" She always says that! thought Alfie.

Dad was soon carving the beef and Mum dished up the roast potatoes and vegetables. Alfie passed the gravy round and he told them about meeting Jimmy the ex-Milkman in the park.

"Yes he's a nice old chap," said his Mum. "He retired soon after we moved here."

"He tells some great tales about when he was in the War," said Alfie, "but he seems a bit sad and lonely." Alfie decided to say hello again next time he saw him.

Eddie begged a piece of beef and a roast potato from Alfie. It was still very hot, and Eddie took it gingerly between his big greedy chompers, then ran out the open back door into the garden to eat it - as it was still too hot to swallow!

Alfie helped his Mum clear away and then he played swing ball in the garden with his Dad. Eddie kept jumping up and trying to grab the ball as they batted it in between each other. He soon tired and he just sat in the shade watching the game.

The afternoon passed and after reading his comic and

watching some television it was Alfie's bedtime. He had soon changed into his pyjamas, cleaned his teeth and jumped into bed. Eddie jumped up with him and soon they were both snoring away.

The Dakota engines roared as the plane taxied down the runway for take off. The heavily armed soldiers in the back (and one dog) braced themselves as it lurched into the air in the dark moonless night.

Corporal Alfie and his sniffer dog, Eddie, and the commando unit were off on a sabotage mission behind enemy lines. Corporal Alfie tightened up his parachute straps before checking Eddie's harness and backpack. It was a special canvas jacket made for Eddie that had numerous small pockets and useful items in it.

The soldiers stared at each other across the aircraft as the French coast slipped beneath them. Their faces were smeared black and they had all had been briefed on their mission to attack a secret enemy communications centre, hidden in a large wood some ten miles from the coast.

The red "Ready" light came on and they all hooked their parachutes to the rail and stood facing the now open door. The red light changed to green and soon they were all jumping out of the back door. Corporal Alfie and Eddie jumped together. The line tugged and their parachute opened. They were drifting down into the inky blackness. A gust of wind caught them and they drifted to the right. Corporal Alfie could just make out the ground as it headed swiftly towards them. He bent his legs and as he hit the ground he rolled over. He jumped up and swiftly removed their harnesses before rolling the harnesses and parachutes up. Whilst he worked, Eddie dug a hole for Corporal Alfie to bury the rolled up pack - they were to leave no trace of their presence.

Corporal Alfie and Eddie reported to Sergeant Jimmy who was leading the unit. Sergeant Jimmy took a quick headcount and found that one man was missing. Corporal Alfie sent Eddie off to look for the missing private, because that's what he was trained to do. Eddie searched and was gone for about five minutes. When he returned he tugged Corporal Alfie in to the wood at the side of the landing field. The missing man was hanging from a tree, stuck by his parachute. He was too high to get down on his own. Corporal Alfie climbed the tree and cut the man down.

"Thanks for getting me down," said the Private.

"We're a team and we must all stick together," said Sergeant Jimmy. "Now lets all get on with the job!"

They checked their map and found that they were right beside the wood where the communication centre was hidden. "Smack on target! Great! I hate too much walking!" said Sergeant Jimmy.

Corporal Alfie let Eddie go in front in the darkness. Suddenly Eddie froze and he showed Corporal Alfie a trip wire that led to a type of anti-personnel mine that jumped up into the air before it exploded. The mine was safely defused and all the men realised that Eddie had probably saved most of their lives.

The men continued towards the centre but after about half an hour of searching they couldn't find it. They were about to start another sweep of the wood when Eddie's nostrils started twitching. He could smell breakfast cooking somewhere! He led the commando unit towards the smell from a smoking chimney.

He led them right across the other side of the wood and then he dropped flat, without a sound. This indicated that the enemy was close by. Corporal Alfie saw a bright red cigarette end as the enemy guard on duty smoked and leaned against a large concrete door, hidden in a mound of earth and trees.

Sergeant Jimmy crept up on the guard and took him by surprise. The guard fell in a heap as Sergeant Jimmy knocked him out. The commando unit approached the door and gently tried to open it. It was bolted from the inside.

Corporal Alfie scouted around the area and he found an airshaft that fed the underground complex. He had noticed a large hornet nest hanging from a nearby tree. He emptied his backpack and stood underneath the nest; another man cut the stalk at the top of the nest.

The nest fell into the backpack and Corporal Alfie quickly closed the top as tightly as he could. He could hear the buzzing from the nest getting louder and louder as the hornets got angrier. They had to be quick! He ran silently to an airshaft and, letting the top of the rucksack open as he dropped it, he quickly covered the shaft hole with a jacket. He could hear the angry hornets heading towards the light of the complex, and he and his men looked expectantly towards the door of the building.

Within two minutes the door was thrown open and the screaming enemy radio operators came running out to get away from the stinging hornets. The enemy was captured, gagged and tied to the trees.

To get the hornets out from the bunker, Corporal Alfie put a clod of dirt on the smoking chimney. The smoke from the wood stove in the complex soon filled the bunker's interior and the hornets all left. Corporal Alfie then took the dirt off the chimney and whilst Corporal Alfie and his men stole the enemy code and signal books, the demolition team moved in and set their charges. They then quickly ran off into the night towards the coast. They were about two miles away when they heard a loud series of small explosions as the complex was put out of action for a long while.

But they also knew that the area was now swarming with the enemy who were looking for the commandos.

Sergeant Jimmy led the men to an old farm barn to hide during the day. The barn was full of hay and straw bales. The soldiers quickly built a false wall of bales and sheltered behind it. Corporal Alfie and Eddie took the first guard watch, as the exhausted commandos slept.

An enemy lorry stopped outside, enemy soldiers jumped out and began searching the buildings. The commando unit was on full alert but all were still and silent. The enemy soldiers looked in the barn, saw it was full of bales and went off to search elsewhere. The lorry started up and the enemy was gone.

The commandos stayed in the barn until darkness fell. They were about eight miles from the coast and the submarine that was scheduled to pick them up in three hours time. They were about to leave when the enemy lorry returned. Quickly they all ducked back down again but were relieved to realise that only the driver was in it. They soon overpowered the driver and had taken his uniform and cap.

Sergeant Jimmy, who was the only one who could speak the enemy's language, put on the driver's uniform and cap. "Time to be bold!" he said as they all loaded up into the lorry.

They set off down the road towards the coast and were making good progress until they went round a bend in the road, straight into an enemy roadblock. A barrier was across the road, manned by two guards. They asked Sergeant Jimmy for his driver's pass and he calmly reached in his pocket and gave it to them to inspect.

They glanced at it and then gave it back. They lifted the barrier and waved the lorry through. Sergeant Jimmy laughed as they went on their way. "Boldness pays every time!"

"Sergeant Jimmy has more front than Brighton!" stated Corporal Alfie, and all the men laughed.

The lorry was soon parked up near the coast. The commando unit made their way along the cliff towards a small guard post that overlooked the beach that was their rendezvous point. It was nearly time for them to be taken off the beach.

Sergeant Jimmy flashed a red light out to sea to signal the submarine. A single green flash came back from a small boat some hundred yards out. Unfortunately a Guard noticed the light and raised the alarm. The commandos headed down the beach as fast as they could run as the guard turned on a searchlight and started to sweep the beach with it.

Corporal Alfie pulled the pin out off a grenade and kept the trigger lever down. He got Eddie to hold it in his mouth then hissed "Get away!" Eddie bounded up the cliff path with the grenade held tightly in his mouth. He had been trained to deliver these special presents. He crept up behind the searchlight and dropped it and ran back down towards the beach. The grenade took ten seconds on its slow fuse before it exploded, blowing up the searchlight.

The beach was in darkness again.

Eddie ran back towards Corporal Alfie and jumped into the inflatable boat. "That dog's a hero! He deserves a medal!" said one of the commandos, and all the men agreed. Eddie kept saving their lives.

They paddled like mad and bullets whistled by them in the darkness as the guards fired wildly. They were soon on board the safety of the submarine where everyone fed Eddie with biscuits as he did his best impression of a starving dog.

Back at base there was a special parade and, for a job bravely done, Eddie was presented with a medal as was Corporal Alfie and Sergeant Jimmy

The military band struck up a tune by Busted. "Busted?" said Alfie amazed. "But this is 1944!"

Alfie's clock radio alarm going off to wake him up for school. He shook his head to clear the dreams out of his head before lifting up his pillow to find an enemy driver's cap with the badge still on it, and a medal that Eddie had been given for bravery.

Chapter Nine
Fireballs And Thick Mud

That day at school Alfie and his friends were surprised to see a bright red fire truck parked in the school playground. The classes took it in turns to be shown around the fire engine and they learnt that the firemen called it "The Pump" and they were shown the equipment kept in "The Pump Lockers" and that the large ladder on top was called a "135".

When the ladder was taken down from the pump, the order was to "Slip and pitch". Alfie was amazed at all the equipment that the pump carried - cutting equipment, compressors, first aid and breathing apparatus (known to the fireman as "BA").

"It is all necessary for the firemen so they can cope with any situation that they find themselves up against," explained the Leading Fireman ("LF").

After school lunch the firemen put on a display for the whole school. Firemen ran towards the building reeling out the thick hoses and then putting branches in them to fix smaller hoses to them. They then soaked the side of the school science block, which the children all found quite funny. Ladders were pitched up beside the school and members of the school staff were "Rescued". The children cheered as the headmaster was thrown over the shoulder of a burly fireman and carried down to the ladder to the ground – and several children jokingly chanted for him to be put back!

The fireman had a small metal tray that they set alight. They showed the school how to use a fire extinguisher to put the flames out. They even let several children have a go, including William and Grace.

Then they ran out of extinguishers and the demonstration switched to a display of cutting a roof off a car to get the trapped driver out. Alfie was pleased that he was allowed to have a go with the combi tool as the LF supervised.

The school bell rang for the end of school and Alfie was collected by his Dad, who waited with Alfie as they watched the hoses pipes rolled up and stowed in the pumps lockers. Alfie was keen to baffle his Dad with all the technical terms that he had learnt that afternoon. His Dad said that he hoped Alfie learnt his lessons that well too.

Alfie sat having his tea and telling his mum all about cutting the roof off an old car. "That's nice, dear," said his Mum. "Perhaps you could be a fireman when you grow up!"

As it was a nice bright evening, Dad suggested they all drove to the beach for a long walk. They soon arrived at the beach car park and Alfie noticed that a bright red Pump was parked on the slip with its lights flashing. He could see out in the distance that a group of firemen were standing around looking concerned. They were near a sign that said "Danger Quicksand".

One of the firemen came back to the pump to use the RT (Radio). The tide was about to come in and a man was stuck in the quicksand up to his neck and the firemen couldn't get near enough to save him as they were sinking too. The control room told them to keep trying and did they want a helicopter scrambled to help? The LF told them to stand by whilst he considered the best approach. Alfie asked the LF if he could make a suggestion. "I'm open to all ideas!" said the LF.

Alfie outlined his idea and the LF said it was very clever and might just work. The LF barked orders at his crew.

Alfie stood back with his mum and dad as the firemen opened up the Pump's lockers. They carried a small petrol powered air compressor, short ladder and several lengths of the largest, fattest, hose they had towards the trapped man in the quicksand. The LF got his men to roll two large hoses towards the trapped man so that they were parallel with each other. The far ends had been closed off and the hoses near ends connected to the compressor. The compressor filled the hoses with air and a ladder was put on top of them. The weight was distributed evenly so the fireman didn't sink.

The smallest fireman of Blue Watch crawled along the ladder with a rope that had a loop in the end like a lasso. The loop was placed over the trapped man's head and under his arms.

The tide was just starting to come in as the whole of Blue Watch and Alfie's Dad, pulled the rope like a big tug of war team. The man was gradually inched out of the suction of the sand. He was put on to a stretcher board and taken to a waiting ambulance which took him off to hospital to be checked over. The firemen barely had time to recover their gear and equipment before the whole area was submerged under the incoming tide.

"Well done, Alfie!" said the LF. "That's a new one for the fire training manual!"

The pump was soon packed up and ready to go back to the station house. The LF invited Alfie to come to the station one afternoon and he might get a ride in the pump with its lights flashing and it siren going!

Eddie had waited very patiently to finish his walk and so the family set off along the beach footpath. Eddie chased a rabbit over the dunes and then came back puffing like a train after it had eluded him. He then turned round and walked towards the car; he had had enough!

"Looks like we are being taken for a walk, by Eddie!" said Alfie's Mum.

They were soon home and Alfie was told to go straight to bed as it was getting late.

He brushed his teeth and his Dad came in to see him tucked into bed.

Eddie positioned himself in his huge basket beside Alfie's bed and nodded off. "He's dreaming that one day he might just catch a rabbit!" said his Dad.

"Only in his dreams!" said Alfie as he slipped under his warm duvet.

The heat from the burning oil well was terrific as Alfie "Nitro" Nelson and his team of specialist oil well fire-fighters, bobbed up and down on the North Sea - one hundred and fifty miles offshore.

There had been an explosion on the oil well and it had been alight for two weeks. There was a huge fire and an acrid pall of jet-black smoke was spewing in clouds from the three hundred feet high drilling rig. There were thirty pipes feeding oil from the broken wellheads into the belly of the fire from the seabed reservoirs.

"Nitro" Nelson had been pumping seawater onto the fire for three days from two special ships at the rate of seventy thousand gallons a minute. He needed to cool the glowing metal steelwork before he could use some nitro glycerine to blow out the fire and cap the broken wellhead. They also had to put up with the high winds and the stormy waves that battered the fireboats.

One side of the platform had been cooled enough for two men, in silver asbestos fire suits, to hitch up some of the broken steel work and drag it away from the well head to expose the broken pipes. The fire flared up again as the men backed away. They were being cooled with water hoses played on them by their team. The water turned to steam as it cooled the overheating men.

The men were soon taking a break as "Nitro" Nelson put on his silver fire suit and prepared to go into action. He ordered two fixed water hoses to be trained on the wellhead to carry on cooling the Steelwork as he prepared his charge of nitro glycerine. Then "Nitro" calmly loaded a special metal drum with a measured amount of the high explosive. He wrapped the drum three times in asbestos blanket and wired the detonator into the top of the drum. His men had tied a hose to the crane cable and the drum was fixed on the hook below. The water was turned on to keep the drum cool. "Nitro" Nelson then ordered his men to get back on the ship and prepare to fit the well cap and operate the mud pump.

The steelwork had cooled under the relentless spray of seawater and "Nitro" Nelson, climbed on board the crane. An armoured plate that his men had fixed on had closed off the windows. They had left a narrow slit for "Nitro" to see through. The heat on board the crane was still terrific even though water hoses were aimed at the cab.

"Nitro" took a deep breath and prayed that the steelwork wasn't hot enough to re-ignite the oil if he managed to put the fire out.

"Nitro" pulled the levers on the crane and swung the drum of explosives over the burning wellhead. He eased the drum down until it disappeared into the smoke. He pressed the button and ducked down.

"Kaboom!" The oilrig shook. "Nitro" Nelson and the crane took off backwards a full three feet into the air, before landing on its side. "Nitro" suddenly felt the heat subside and he realised that the fire had been put out.

He pulled himself from the wreckage of the crane although its mast was now missing, and stepped on to the deck. "Whatever we are being paid for this job, it's not enough!" he said, dusting himself down and checking for broken bones. To add insult to injury, he was suddenly showered in a hail of thick black, sticky, crude oil.

His men were running in all directions now that the fire was out. They started fitting blow out prevention caps to the broken pipes with big spanners and began pumping steel balls and thick mud down into them to cap the flow.

"Nitro" Nelson and his fearless team had put the fire out

and saved thousands of gallons of oil being burnt and polluting the North Sea.

"Nitro" Nelson went to walk to the Helicopter pad to be taken off the rig when he found that his boot soles had stuck to the still hot metal deck. He couldn't move!

Alfie could barely breathe as he woke up covered in sweat and wrapped tightly in his duvet. He managed to unwrap himself and felt under his pillow, he found an oilrig wellhead spanner.

Chapter Ten
No Bullets – But a Big Bang!

Alfie sat chewing an apple at afternoon break time. He took a large bite when he felt one of his teeth move. It had started to come loose! He found it hard to concentrate in his maths lesson as he kept wriggling the loose tooth with his tongue.

Mr Morris the teacher noticed Alfie's distraction and asked him to explain Pythagoras's Law to the class! Alfie managed to bluff his way through explaining that the square of the hypotenuse is equal to the sum of the squares on the other two sides.

Mr Morris was very impressed and carried on teaching the class, with diagrams on the blackboard of the classic triangle with sides in proportion of 3:4:5.

Alfie kept wriggling the loose tooth; it was driving him mad.

The school bell rang for the end of day and Alfie was the first one out of the door. That pesky tooth still wouldn't come out although all the wiggling had made it come very loose! Mum and Eddie had come to meet him and he was soon explaining his problem to his Mum. Alfie wanted to make sure that it was out before he went to bed – to ensure that the "Tooth Fairy" would come and give him money that night.

"There is a way to get it out faster," said his Mum. "But you need to be brave!"

When they got home Alfie's mum took some string from her kitchen cupboard and made a small loop at one end. She then got Alfie to open his mouth and she dropped the loop over the loose tooth and tightened it. She gave the loose end of the string to Alfie.

"Go on then, tug it!" she said. Alfie took up the slack but immediately stopped and let go, as the tooth started hurting.

Alfie was pulling all sorts of faces as his Dad came in from work. "Let me pull the string for you!" he volunteered. Alfie's Dad reached for the string but Alfie jumped back and wouldn't let him pull it.

"I know," said Dad "Tie it to the door handle and then slam it!"

Alfie tied the string to the door handle and tried to slam the door. Three times he did it but each time he moved his head closer to the door and the tooth stayed unpulled. Alfie sat all evening watching the telly with a piece of long string hanging out of his mouth. His Dad sat beside him and when Alfie wasn't looking he tied a small chew bone to the end of it.

"Here boy!" Dad called as he dropped the chew bone in Eddie's mouth. Alfie realised too late that the bone was tied to the string. Eddie dashed off into the kitchen to eat the bone and he took the tooth clean out of Alfie's mouth. Alfie never felt a thing.

'Dad's pulled some tricks before, but this is the worst!' thought Alfie as he rescued the valuable tooth from the kitchen floor. He wrapped it in tissue paper and placed it under his pillow. This makes a change, he thought, for me to be putting stuff under my pillow! Alfie climbed into bed and the deep white softness enveloped him.

The headphones crackled into life. "Calling Red Leader! This is Green Area Command."

"Green Area Command! This is Red Leader," replied Wing Commander Alfie.

"Red Leader! Bandits at Angels 150! Sixteen miles south of your position!"

"Roger," said Wing commander Alfie as he opened the throttle on his Spitfire. The Merlin Engine strained its entire horsepower and Red Leader pulled the stick back and sent his plane into a steep ascent. His two wingmen followed in formation, up into the clouds and through to seventeen thousand feet. The sun burst into their cockpits as they broke through the clouds. There, less than two miles away and on a course for London, were six enemy bombers.

"Red leader to flight! Tally Ho!"

"Prepare to peel and attack - now!"

The three Spitfires swooped down on the enemy bombers and opened fire. The machine gunners on the bombers opened up and the sky was full of red-hot tracer shells as the planes neared.

Wing Commander Alfie lined a bomber up in his sights and pressed the gun button on his joystick. A stream of lead slammed into the tail of one bomber and it spun to the side and dived toward the earth. Its crew were bailing out and a stream of parachutes slowly followed the stricken plane down.

The wingmen shot down a bomber each and reformed just in time, as a wing of enemy fighter escort planes bore down on them from out of the sun. The sky was soon full of vapour trails as the Spitfires engaged the enemy fighter planes. Wing Commander Alfie shot down another bomber and one of his wingmen shot down a fighter plane. The enemy fighters pulled away from the fight and took off back towards France. This was because the size of their fuel tanks could only give them about ten minutes over the target area.

"Red Leader to Green area Command, we are returning to base - job done!"

"Roger that, Red Leader. Well done!"

Suddenly Wing Commander Alfie saw a fast moving Doodlebug (a flying bomb) pass under him. He gained height and pushed the Spitfire joystick forward into a shallow dive to build up speed. The doodlebugs were powered by a jet engine and could fly very fast, but a diving Spitfire in full throttle could catch up.

The Merlin engine roared as the Spitfire swooped and came up behind the flying bomb. Wing Commander Alfie pressed the firing button on his joystick but his guns only fired about three times before he found that he was out of bullets. He could see the empty cornfields below were starting to change to housing and London was only about fifteen miles away.

What could he do to stop it? Lives would be lost.

Red Leader coolly opened the throttle wide open and flew alongside the doodlebug.

He inched his starboard wing under the port wing of the flying bomb and gradually lifted his wing up. Just as the wings made contact Wing Commander Alfie gave the doodlebug a short sharp lift and flipped it up and over. The doodlebug spun downward in a spiral flight of doom. The flying bomb hit the open countryside and blew a hole some twenty feet deep in the middle of a grass field.

"Better there than in the centre of London!" said one of Red Leader's wingmen.

"Although I bet some farmer won't be happy!" said the other wingman into this radio.

"Home chaps," said Wing Commander Alfie as he turned for Biggin Hill airfield.

As the Spitfires landed men started to form up ready to refuel and rearm them.

Wing Commander Alfie undid his parachute harness and climbed out of the cockpit of his trusty Spitfire. Underneath the cockpit windows on the fuselage, his aircraft fitter was about to paint the outlines of another two kills, when his wingman suggested that he ought to start another line for Wing Commander Alfie's Doodlebugs!

Red Leader had just sat down in the airfield Ready Room to enjoy a cup of "Rosie lee", when the alarm bell rang.

"Red flight! Scramble, Scramble, Scramble! Enemy sighted!"

Alfie jumped out of bed and was on the stair landing before he realised he was awake.

Eddie looked at him as if he were mad, as Alfie came back into the bedroom and climbed into bed, rubbing the sleep out of his eyes. He looked under his pillow to find an RAF pilot wings badge and a fifty pence piece from the tooth fairy!

Chapter Eleven
The Slip-Up

It was a Saturday and Alfie's Mum went off to work at The Beach café. Alfie was staying at home with his Dad for a change as Grace had gone to see her Grandparents for the weekend and William was out as well.

Alfie played with Eddie until Eddie refused to fetch the ball back anymore and he slumped down beside Alfie's Dad in his chair. Alfie's dad was reading The Daily Bugle and moaning about the shares and his pension value going down, none of which meant anything to Alfie - although he tried to look interested.

Alfie had the fifty pence from the tooth fairy and his two pound allowance burning a hole in his pocket. He took his Dad a cup of tea and asked if they could go to the shops after lunch to spend his money.

"Ok, young man," Dad said. After a baked potato with cheese and salad, Alfie quickly cleared the table and put the dishes in the dishwasher.

"I don't know who's more keen to go!" said his Dad, as Eddie appeared with the dog lead in his mouth and dropped it at Alfie's dad's feet. "Looks like I'm being ganged up on, so let's go."

They all walked together down the road to the park. Eddie went racing across the grass to meet a small white Scottie dog and Alfie's Dad sat on a bench in the sunshine.

Alfie said goodbye to his Dad and promised to be home at teatime. He headed for the shops and was soon looking through the shop windows at the displays. He went into the newsagents and bought a comic book and some wrapped toffees and some polo mints.

He was walking past the fire station when he saw that the firemen were cleaning their Pump.

"Hello Alfie, and how are you?" said a voice.

Alfie turned round and saw that it was the LF that he had met on the beach rescue. "Would you like to look around and help clean the pump?" said Leading Fireman Hutton.

"Yes please LF!" said Alfie. Soon Alfie was polishing the bright red Pump and tidying up the inside of the cab with a brush and dustpan. Alfie joined the firemen in the mess for a cup of tea and a slice of fruitcake. LF Hutton asked Alfie if he would like a ride in the Pump, as they going to take it to the main fire station in town to leave it for a service. They could drop Alfie off at his home in Acacia Avenue as it was on the way.

Alfie jumped at the chance and he sat in the back of the cab as it set off out of the station. They had gone only a short distance when the RT (Radio) burst into life and the pump and crew were ordered to attend a call from a member of the public. A man had seen a cow in Farmer Appleton's field and it was stuck. The lights came on and the siren wailed as the pump sped towards Top End Farm. "Sit still, young Alfie!" said LF Hutton.

The crew arrived at the field gate and one fireman jumped out and opened the gate for the pump to drive in. The firemen laughed at first when they saw the problem. At one end of the sloping field an old iron bathtub had been set in the slope with a small stream flowing gently in and out of it, which was designed to give. Farmer Appleton's cows some fresh water to drink. There on its back, stuck in the tub with its legs in the air was a Jersey Cow! It was stuck fast and couldn't move.

One fireman joked, "It must have slipped on the soap."

"Cut that out. It's not funny!" said LF Hutton.

The firemen soon opened the lockers and were working

out how to get the cow out of the bathtub. They erected a metal tripod over the cow and affixed a block and tackle with straps. They then found that the straps couldn't be put around the cow as it was wedged tight into the tub.

Alfie meanwhile was feeding the cow a couple of polo mints to keep it quiet. The firemen were stumped. Alfie thought very hard and then he asked the LF if he could make a suggestion.

"Why not lad, we're not having much luck! And you do seem to be pretty inventive with your ideas." LF Hutton said, remembering the last time Alfie had helped them.

Alfie had seen a long length of thick fence post beside the gate and Alfie suggested that the firemen put one end underneath the bathtub and raise the other end as a lever. After a bit of puffing by the firemen the bath tub and cow rolled gently over, the cow stood up and the tub dropped off.

"Well done Alfie! Another one for the manual – '*How to get cows out of bathtubs*'," said the LF. "Although I don't think that the town fire service would ever have to use it!"

The firemen loaded the gear back up and within five minutes were dropping Alfie off outside his house. Alfie's Dad was asleep in the front garden in a deck chair and so didn't notice the Pump draw up. All the neighbours were looking as the cheeky driver set the siren off. Alfie's Dad woke up with a start and fell out of his deck chair. The firemen all laughed as they drove off. Alfie tried hard not to laugh too, but his Dad soon saw the funny side of it and they were both almost crying with laughter as Alfie told him about the episode of the cow stuck in the bathtub!

Alfie's Mum thought it was pretty funny too when she got home!

They had just finished tea when there was a knock at the door. It was Farmer Appleton. He had come to thank Alfie for helping to get his cow out of the bathtub, and invited them all over for Sunday lunch. He said that even Eddie could come.

"See you tomorrow, then, oh, and if young Alfie wants to come about ten, he can help me feed the cattle and pigs." Farmer Appleton left and Alfie's Mum told Alfie it was time for bed.

Alfie was talking to Eddie on the bed. He was telling Eddie all about the next day and how Eddie had to behave around the farm animals and not chase them. His Mum came in and gave Alfie a hug and a kiss goodnight. She turned the light out in the diver's helmet and left the door just a little ajar. A thin beam from the landing light cut across the gloom.

The light changed from red to blue as it swept across Ambassador Alfie's body and he felt himself being lifted up into the air and towards the flying saucer. His silver button had called him to come to the middle of a field for a meeting with the aliens.

He was soon inside the ship and it seemed to be enormous on the inside yet quite small on the outside.

The head alien, called Galex, smiled and beamed a thought to Ambassador Alfie. He said, "That's why it's called a space ship!" Ambassador Alfie laughed and the atmosphere became very friendly.

The flying saucer zoomed upwards and parked itself on the edge of the Earth's atmosphere. The view from the windows was terrific. Ambassador Alfie took in the entire world as it revolved below him.

Galex had summoned Ambassador Alfie for vital talks – or rather, thoughts.

"We have been visiting the Earth for many centuries," said Galex, "and we are worried that man is polluting the planet. Our own planet was exactly the same and we had to clean it up, but it is now dying due to its age, we expect it to explode and destroy itself in a few years time."

Ambassador Alfie asked what the people of Earth could do to help.

Galex said that his people wished to move to Earth and live in the deep trench parts of the Oceans. He offered to help clean up the Earth using their advanced technology in exchange for being allowed to live there. Ambassador Alfie need not worry, as they would never be seen because they would live at such depths. They hated the light and so the deeper the better.

Ambassador Alfie agreed as long as he could contact them, if he needed to, with his silver button communicator. Galex shook his hand in agreement and landed the Flying saucer in a field near Ambassador Alfie's house. The Flying saucer took off silently and disappeared into the night sky with a loud bark. Bark?

Alfie woke up to see Eddie at the window with his head under the curtains barking at the cat next door.

Chapter Twelve
A Circle of Wheat

Alfie looked under his pillow to find a set of engineering drawings for an atmosphere scrubber in the language of Galex. Alfie held the silver button as he looked at it and understood it perfectly. He put it in his drawer until he would find someone able to make it. He let Eddie out into the garden but the cat was long gone.

He washed, dressed in his farming clothes, as he explained to his Mum, and ate breakfast. He fed Eddie breakfast and then he took him for a good walk.

He timed his arrival at Top End farm perfectly. Farmer Appleton was just leaving the farmhouse and pulling his bright red braces up over his check shirt. "Morning young master Nelson" he said. "I hope that you are ready for some work?"

"Oh yes," said Alfie keenly.

Alfie tied Eddie's lead to a post in the shade, where Eddie could see him as he helped the farmer. Eddie flopped down and kept a weather eye on the chickens that were walking around the farmyard, flicking his gaze to Alfie every now and again.

Farmer Appleton walked into the yard and picked up a pitchfork. He walked towards a stack of huge hay bales, weighing several hundredweight each, and pretended that he was going to show Alfie how to pick one up, put it on his shoulder and walk to the field. Alfie looked amazed, knowing he wasn't strong enough to pick one of them up. "I'm only joking," laughed Farmer Appleton, getting into his tractor cab.

Before long Alfie was opening and closing the field gates

as the farmer picked up the giant hay bales with his forklift tractor. Alfie peeled off the plastic wrapping and then cut the strings keeping the bales together. The bales dropped into the large feed racks in the field and the cattle all crowded round and started to tug the fresh hay through the bars and munch on it. They then put out some fresh salt licks and cleaned out the water troughs.

The morning flew by and soon Alfie's Mum and Dad arrived with Alfie's smart clothes. Alfie got changed and joined everybody in the dining room. His eyes nearly fell out of their sockets when he saw that Mrs Appleton had cooked the biggest Sunday lunch he had ever seen.

"I hope that you have worked up an appetite," she said as she shovelled a heap of vegetables beside the thick slices of beef that her husband had carved off the joint.

The adults were chatting away as Alfie manfully attacked the plateful. He finished it all up and was feeling rather full as Mrs Appleton spooned some more vegetables, Yorkshire pudding, beef and a dollop of gravy on his plate.

"The boy's hungry!" she said. "Needs feeding after all that work."

"Leave space for some pudding, Alfie," said Farmer Appleton.

Alfie was about to burst as he finished the last spoonful of Cream Caramel.

All Alfie wanted to do was sit down and sleep but his Dad and Farmer Appleton wanted to go for a walk. Eddie finished a few scraps of beef from the lunch and he pulled excitedly on his lead as they all walked along the footpath beside the grass fields and the corn fields of Top End farm.

"Here are my pedigree sheep, and over here are my Jersey cows and their followers - their calves," explained Farmer Appleton as they walked. "Over the next rise is my champion wheat crop."

The walkers arrived at the next field to see Farmer Appleton struck dumb as they all saw an enormous crop circle. It was obviously the very spot where the flying saucer had dropped Earth Ambassador Alfie off the night before.

The circle was over fifty feet across and covered in wonderful geometric shapes. It looked fantastic although the champion wheat crop was totally flattened in places.

"Those blasted jokers from the village pub, I expect!" said an angry Farmer Appleton.

"Unless you believe in Aliens?" said Alfie. Farmer Appleton scoffed at the thought.

"It's them jokers!" he repeated.

They all walked back to the farmhouse and said their goodbyes to Farmer Appleton and his wife.

"Alfie can come and help anytime he likes," said Farmer Appleton. "He was a lot of help this morning. I could use a lad like him on the farm over the school holidays - paid, of course".

Alfie told his Mum and Dad that he would quite like to help the farmer as he enjoyed feeding the cattle. But he would need a pair of Wellingtons, as the one's that Farmer Appleton lent him were a bit big! Eddie sat by the front gate and waited for them to open it for him. He was thinking that it was teatime and he was hungry as usual, whereas Alfie didn't think he would be able to eat again for days!

Alfie's Mum opened a tin of dog food for him and Eddie bolted it down. "Just like feeding the pigs at the farm, the way he's troughing into that food," said Alfie.

Chapter Thirteen
Saving Dinner!

There were only repeats and soaps on the television so Alfie went to bed early and started to read a book about Robinson Crusoe. Alfie also had his radio on and he listened to the chart show as he read.

"Alfie! Will you turn that row down!" called his Dad.

"Ok Dad," replied Alfie. "I'm going to sleep now as all that farming has tired me out."

The sea lapping gently at his face caused Robinson Alfie to come round.

His ship had hit the rocks in a huge storm and had floundered. It was calm now and the sea was as level as a sheet of glass. Rubbing the salt and sand from his eyes he stood up and wiped himself down. Looking out to sea he could see the mast of the ship sticking out of the water. All around him were bits of broken and smashed ships timbers.

He was totally alone. The sea had taken all of his shipmates.

He looked around and realised that he was on a small island, covered in coconut trees and lush green jungle. He picked up bits and pieces off the beach that he thought might help him to survive and heaped them above the high tide mark. While it was so calm he swam out to the ship and managed to dive down and salvage a lot of useful items. Then to speed things up he managed to make a small raft and used it to dive from and ferry the salvaged goods back to shore. His best find was a chest of tools that belonged to the ships carpenter and a musket, gunpowder barrels, fuses and a bag of shot from the ships armoury.

The light was going as Robinson Alfie tied some canvas sail between three coconut trees. He cracked open a coconut with the carpenter's small axe and ate the white flesh. He heaped up some green leaves and, exhausted, he lay down to sleep.

The next morning he awoke refreshed, and decided to explore the island. He needed to find clean water to drink and see if he could find better shelter. He set off for the highest point and after an hour of climbing he reached the top. He could see the entire island below him and he could look out to sea for miles but all he saw were the ocean and the reef with the waves washing over it. He went back towards the beach using another rocky way down and, noticing a small opening in the rocks, he found a cave.

It was dark inside but as his eyes grew accustomed to the dimness he saw that it was large enough to make into a long-term shelter: Robinson Alfie had no idea how long it would be before he was rescued.

At the top was a small opening that let in the light and would also make a good chimney if he could make a fire. Part of the wall at the back had a glisten to it and Robinson Alfie discovered that a small drop of water was constantly dripping from it. Robinson Alfie put half a coconut shell under the drip to collect the water. It soon filled the shell and he was able to drink the fresh cool water.

The rest of the day was spent fitting out the cave with bits from the ship. He cut down some tall bamboo canes and used some thin creepers to lash them together making a table, a chair and a bed. He piled some big rocks in a ring, made a small heap of dried grass and shaved some wood to put shavings in the centre. He then made a small sharp stick and cut a groove in a thick piece of wood. He rubbed the stick back and forth on the groove and, after a lot of effort that made him sweat, the wood at the tip of the stick started to smoke from the friction.

Robinson Alfie put the small smoking stick on to the dried grass and shavings and began to blow gently. The embers glowed red and the smoke got thicker and thicker. Suddenly the grass caught fire and he heaped small sticks and then thicker logs until he had a warming fire going. The smoke went up and out of the skylight chimney.

Robinson Alfie was pleased with himself now he had fire, water and shelter. Tomorrow he would have to hunt for food, he thought as he settled down for the night.

Outside he could hear the wind howling as he slept comfortably in his nice warm cave.

The next morning he looked out to sea and saw that the ship's mast had gone and there was more driftwood and wreckage on the beach. Again he salvaged what he could, before setting off into the thick vegetation to look for food. He found a tree covered in bright red berries and he cautiously tried one – as you have to be careful with some berries! It looked all right but it tasted terrible and burnt his mouth. He spat it out, and washed his mouth out with water, and kept looking.

His luck changed for the better as he spotted a banana plant with a big hand of bananas hanging down. He cut it down and as he carried it back he found a nut tree. He picked some of the nuts and put them in his small cloth loin bag.

Later, after eating his banana and nut lunch, Robinson Alfie searched the rock pools at the beach. He took with him, an old metal bucket that he had salvaged and used for cooking. He darted here and there, lifting up the small rocks where he found limpets that he prised from the rocks with his knife. He also found two crabs that snapped at him as he dropped them in his bucket. 'And that is tea taken care of,' he thought proudly.

Back in the cave Robinson Alfie had marked the wall with a piece of chalky rock to count the days. Each day he put another mark. Soon the marks totalled up to over one hundred.

'One hundred days!' thought Robinson Alfie to himself. 'Will I never get off this island?'

His only friend was a parrot that he had half tamed with the bribery of fruit and nuts. He spent his days, every day the same, gathering food and planting fruit and nut seeds all over the island to keep his supply going. He had managed to make a harpoon from the tools he'd salvaged from the ship, and his fishing was getting better - occasionally he managed to spear a fish or catch a crayfish to eat. He had a musket but there was nothing to shoot.

He was just going back into his cave when he thought that he heard voices from the beach. Robinson Alfie crept towards the sounds and peered carefully through the green branches. It was voices! And people!

They looked fierce with bones through their noses and they carried white bleached skulls on top of poles. They had arrived in several large sea-going canoes, which were drawn up the beach. They lit fires and it soon became clear to Robinson Alfie that they were cannibals. He decided to stay hidden, then he saw what all their excitement and activity was about.

A man was tied up near the canoes and it was plain from the way he was treated that he was the main course on the cannibal's menu! Robinson Alfie dashed back to the cave and got his musket, shot and a horn of gunpowder. He also took several fused coconuts filled with gunpowder, some small pebbles and a glowing stick from the cave's fire, which he extinguished to stop any smoke being seen.

He crept through the undergrowth until he was the far side of the cannibals. He placed the fused coconuts on top of a small rock in front of his position and waited. Perhaps they would go away without any trouble?

The cannibals danced around their fire and soon it was time to get their dinner ready. The man was dragged forward by a neck rope and was just about to be killed when Robinson Alfie, using his glowing stick, lit the fuse on the first coconut bomb. He threw it down the beach towards the water. The bomb blew up with the loudest bang imaginable. Pebbles shot everywhere and the cannibals turned tail and fled for their canoes.

They left their captive tied up on the beach as they paddled out to sea as fast as they could. Robinson Alfie threw several more bombs from his concealed hiding place as the terrified cannibals kept going. They had never seen anything like it, and probably thought the end of the world had come!

Robinson Alfie ran out of his hiding place and quickly cut the terrified captive free and led him to the cave. He hoped that the cannibals wouldn't come back as they were very superstitious and had had a terrible fright – but he could not be sure! They might become brave in their anger at being deprived of their dinner!

The freed captive gratefully ate the bananas that Robinson Alfie gave him. He started to bow to Robinson Alfie and, in sign language, he said that he thought Alfie was the God of Thunder!

That night they kept watch in case the cannibals returned. Robinson Alfie tried to teach him some English. The native man couldn't get Robinson Alfie to pronounce his name properly so Robinson Alfie decided to call him Lazy-Bones. Lazy-Bones?

"Get up, lazy-bones. It's time for school," his mother was saying, shaking him gently. Alfie jumped from his bed as his mother left the room, and he quickly checked the wardrobe and under the bed for lurking cannibals! Then he looked under his pillow to find a smooth shiny pebble.

Chapter Fourteen
After Bigger Fish!

It was sports day at school and all morning Alfie's class were helping to get the playing field ready for the games. There was lots of preparation but the children all loved being involved. Some children put up ropes for the different races, helping the groundsman to measure out the various distances and put in winning posts; other children set up sideshow tables and pinned paper tablecloths to them, whilst others blew up balloons and tied bunting flags around the field.

They were all exhausted after such hectic activity, and Alfie felt that he had already competed in all the sports events after they finished moving the gym equipment for the junior display.

"Well done, class!" said Mr Morris proudly, after they had finished. "Let's have some lunch."

Alfie, William and Grace queued up in the school canteen for lunch. Butch and his gang pushed past them. "Ready to eat my dust later, you little squits?" said Butch.

"Dream on, food-monster!" muttered William, and Alfie and Grace snickered.

The lunch today was very good and William was thinking of going back for another portion. Alfie managed to stop him as it had just given him an idea. He encouraged Butch, Eric and Murdoch to have extra portions too, even offering them extra cartons of milk to drink. Grace and William hid their laughter, realising that all that extra food and milk would slow them all down in the races. Alfie winked at Grace as he encouraged Butch to have a third portion.

"Jolly good, isn't it?" he said to Grace and William, within Butch's hearing. "I think I might have another portion, if there's enough. I think everyone's going back for more."

"Yes!" said Butch. "But there's only enough for us, you worm! Get out of our way!"

Alfie watched as Butch finished all the food… looking just like one of Farmer Appleton's pigs.

Later that afternoon the three friends lined up against their arch enemies. Butch did a pretend victory dance before the race began. But after about fifty yards of running, Butch clutched his side, howling in pain. Eric and Murdoch quickly followed suite, all bent over double.

Alfie, Grace and William swept past the bigger boys and came in one, two, and three. The same result happened in the sack race. Butch, Eric and Murdoch were taken off to see the Matron.

"Matron's favourite cure for stomach ache is a giant spoonful of cod liver oil!" said Alfie, and the three friends all guffawed with laughter.

Alfie's Mum and Dad clapped as the headmaster presented the three friends with book tokens as their prizes. After their races were all over Alfie went around the small stalls, set up to raise money for the school funds. He won a bottle of pop on the tombola stall and he bought a large slice of creamed sponge cake to eat. He was just about to eat it when he saw Butch come out of the first aid section.

"Like a piece of cake Butch? It's jolly good!"

Butch swore at him and was promptly cuffed around the head by his stern looking Mother.

"Alfie's only trying to be polite," she said. "No need for that bad language!"

Alfie smirked, and went off to tell William and Grace.

"A pretty good day's work, stitching up Butch twice," agreed William.

Alfie waved good-bye to Grace and William and walked

home with his parents, thinking about the book token and what he would spend it on. He thought that he would like to get an adventure book. He had seen one on his last trip to the bookstore, all about a man who went up the Amazon to find a long lost relative.

Alfie's Dad tucked him in for the night and sat on the end of his bed talking to him about helping the farmer in the holidays. Eddie jumped up on the bed too and Alfie stroked him between the ears which sent Eddie all silly and relaxed. Eddie was soon fast asleep and Alfie's Dad thought that Alfie ought to be as well. Alfie snuggled down in his duvet and was sucked down into the softness of the mattress.

Down and down, he was falling rapidly in the darkness, until the sharp jerk of his parachute opening slowed his descent. Eddie was hanging from his harness as the newly promoted Sergeant Alfie braced himself for landing. The pair landed in a soft patch of dirt and rolled over.

Getting up, Sergeant Alfie wiped himself and Eddie down and buried his parachute in the ground. His small unit of men assembled around him as he checked the bearings on his map.

"Check your weapons men," ordered Sergeant Alfie, as he started to lead the way with Eddie. Eddie had his harness on so he knew that he was on search duty. His nose sniffed the ground like a small Hoover. As they neared the rocky outcropthat was to be their observation post, Eddie stopped and stared at the soil. He had found an enemy anti-personnel mine. Sergeant Alfie slowly pushed his long bayonet under the mine and lifted it gently to one side. Corporal William then defused it.

Progress was slow in the dark but soon they were digging in amongst the rocks and hiding their position with camouflage nets and tree branches. As the sun came up they could see across the terrain for miles. Sergeant Alfie radioed HQ to tell them he was in position.

A small cloud of dust was seen in the distance. Sergeant Alfie trained his binoculars on it. He saw an enemy convoy heading west down the forest road. The convoy was led by an officer in a staff car and behind him followed a tank and a lorry carrying troops.

Sergeant Alfie's men were ready to fire but he signalled them silently to stay hidden, as the officer was just a lowly lieutenant. Alfie wanted to catch a bigger fish! The convoy passed by on its way to enemy headquarters. Sergeant Alfie thought that they had better prepare an ambush – although he had hoped he would not to have to take on a tank.

Leaving two men on guard, he instructed the other three men on what he wanted to them to do, now he knew the road that the enemy was using.

They worked silently for several hours picking the spot and putting the plan in place. Sergeant Alfie had just taken a drink when Eddie sat bolt upright and looked down the road. A car was coming down the forest road. Sergeant Alfie saw through his binoculars that it had a grand pennant on the bonnet. It was the General! The big fish that he was after!

"This is it men!" he said. "Radio HQ for the helicopter to be ready to pick us up in about thirty minutes, and give them the co-ordinates."

The car approached their position as Sergeant Alfie gave the signal. A small explosion caused a tall tree to fall across the road and block the cars path. The car screeched to a halt and as it tried to reverse, a second charge felled a tree behind - it was trapped! Sergeant Alfie's men sprang up from their hiding place beside the road and had captured the enemy General and his driver without a shot being fired.

The Corporal buried three mines that he had re-armed from the night before, placing them about fifty yards in the road ahead of the road block.

"Shame to waste them!" he said with a grin. They were just loading up into the helicopter when they heard the mines exploding. An enemy lorry full of soldiers had raced down the road to investigate the explosions and had hit the mines the Corporal had left.

Eddie sat beside the enemy General in the helicopter and tried to look tough and growled at him from time to time, baring his teeth to show he meant business!

Sergeant Alfie and his unit had done well and had captured one of the enemy's leaders for interrogation.

"Excellent work, Sergeant!" said Captain Morris. "At this rate you'll be a Major and you'll outrank *me*!"

"I said, I've made you a cup of *tea*," said Alfie's Mum, as she put it beside his diver's helmet lamp.

Alfie finished his cup of tea and looked under his pillow to find a set of Commando Sergeant Stripes. He pushed Eddie off the bed because he was lying across his legs and where Eddie had been lying, was the enemy General's cap badge.

Chapter Fifteen
Stopping The Clock

Alfie was looking forward to going to school today as it was only a half day and then term ended for the summer holidays. And they never did any work on the last day.

Instead, the morning was taken up with tidying up their things and putting them in boxes, ready to move to a new classroom in the new term in September. When the school bell rang for the end of term, Alfie, William and Grace had decided to spend the afternoon together and take Eddie for a walk to see the corn circle in Farmer Appleton's wheat field.

They all went to Alfie's house to dump their school gear and collect Eddie for the walk, before setting off to the wheat field. William and Grace were amazed at the beauty of the crop circle.

"It's so complicated," breathed William.

"It looks like a Spirograph drawing," said Grace. Alfie told them all about Galex and the drawings he had left him.

"That sounds like a job for my uncle Ted; he makes all sorts of things in his shed," said William. "He's on holiday at the moment, but he's back soon."

They all sat under a tree in the shade as it was an unusually hot day, and drank some lemonade - and fed Eddie the cake that Alfie's Mum had given them.

Alfie told them that Farmer Appleton had said that he could help him with the harvest and feed the animals over the holidays – and that he would also be paid!

"Sounds great!" said William. "I don't suppose I could help out too?"

Alfie said he could ask but he didn't hold out much hope as he was experienced and William wasn't.

"Everyone will be earning money but me," moaned William, as Grace was helping her dad at the beach café during the summer. So Alfie promised to ask.

William offered to show them where his uncle Ted lived on the way home. As they came up to the big house and grounds, William noticed a giant removal van parked at the side of the house and two men were quietly loading all of uncle Ted's furniture and possessions in the back of it.

"Funny! He's not back till next week and he never mentioned moving!" said William puzzled.

"Let's get a bit nearer," Alfie suggested, suspecting that all was not what it seemed.

Eddie and Grace stayed back well out of sight, as the two boys crept through the bushes towards the back of the removal van.

"Should get a good price for all this lot," said one of the men.

"Keep it buttoned and get on," the other man replied. "We want to get done and away before anybody notices."

"They're pinching my uncle's stuff!" hissed William to Alfie.

Before Alfie could stop him, William jumped up and ran towards the men, asking them what they were doing. The two men bundled William inside the house and locked him in a cupboard below the stairs which they had just emptied.

Alfie kept his head down as he dashed back to Grace and Eddie. He told Grace to go to the phone box and call the police as Uncle Ted's house was being robbed. Alfie crept back to the house, just as the men were telling William to stop shouting and keep quiet or else! He noted down the vehicle registration in case the men suddenly drove off.

Alfie waited for his moment. The men were distracted for only a minute but that was enough time for Alfie to act. He ran over and opened the driver's door of the removal van and stole the ignition keys. He then ran back and hid back in the undergrowth as the men carried on loading the van. The men walked out with a silver candlestick in each hand, put it in the back of the van and shut the doors.

The two men got in the cab and the driver started to search his pockets for the keys.

"Come on, where are the keys? What have you done with them?" said one of the robbers.

"You had them. Search your pockets properly!" snapped the other.

Suddenly a police car sped into the drive with its horn blowing and blue light flashing. The two men made a run for it but the game was up. They had been caught red handed!

A large policeman rugby-tackled one of the robbers whilst his partner leapt after the other robber. The two men were handcuffed and put in the back seat of the police car.

Alfie and Grace let William out of the understair cupboard. The police told him that it was brave but a bit silly of him to confront the robbers.

"These men have been regularly stealing from houses while people are away on holiday," said one of the policemen. "We have been after these criminals for some time."

"And Uncle Ted's still got his furniture to come home to," said William happily.

Another police car turned up and Alfie, William and Grace had to give statements about what they saw. Alfie's Mum nearly died with shock as a police car drew up in front of her house with Alfie and Eddie in the back.

"What ever have you done now?" she said to Alfie. She calmed down when the policeman told her that Alfie hadn't been arrested. He told her that Alfie had kept the burglars from driving off by taking their van keys and that he was a clever young man.

The police car was just driving away as Alfie's Dad came home from work. It was all explained to him that Alfie wasn't

the mastermind behind a big robbery! He had indeed stopped one!

Eddie was just pleased to be home as he was late for his tea - he was still hungry despite eating all the cake in the field.

Alfie gave a blow-by-blow account of the robbery to his Mum and Dad over tea.

"Lucky we had Grampy and Gran to stay when we went away or we could have come back to an empty house too," said Dad.

"Not with the fearless and very alert Eddie living here!" joked Alfie as Eddie snored, lying on the front room carpet and oblivious to everything.

Alfie was in bed reading as his Mum told him to put the light out. He needed an early night as he was going to help Farmer Appleton next day and he had to be well rested. Alfie was about to go to sleep when his Mum came in again.

"Oh I forgot. I bought a present for you when I was shopping," she said, producing a large pair of green Wellington boots. "I'll leave them at the end of the bed," she added, and went off down the stairs.

Alfie jumped out of bed and tried them on. He walked around the bedroom and thought that they felt just right. He took them off, climbed into bed and snuggled down under the duvet. Downstairs the telephone rang.

Commander Alfie of New Scotland Yard bomb disposal squad answered it.

"Hello, yes! Where? OK be there in less than ten minutes." said Commander Alfie as he picked up his small roll of tools and instruments and dashed out the door.

The blue light was flashing and the horn sounding as the police motorcyclist scythed through the heavy London traffic, with Commander Alfie of the yard hanging on the back!

The motorcycle pulled up in front of the bus station. A police cordon had been thrown around the whole area and the public was being moved well back. A telephone warning had been given that a bomb was planted on a bus in the Bus Terminal, stating that it would go off at eleven o clock. A man had been seen acting suspiciously and had been detained by a policeman who had just been alerted to the threat.

Commander Alfie and his men started to search the buses as the man was being questioned in a back room at the bus station. The man was wearing a wig and false moustache - which were removed before his picture was taken and sent to New Scotland yard for identification checks.

The Bus Terminal was right beside a petrol station and had a large gas tank behind it. If the bomb went off, half of London could go up. The man stubbornly refused to talk.

Commander Alfie suddenly spotted a panel on one of the buses that had not been screwed on properly. Gingerly he unscrewed the panel and carefully started to remove it, carefully checking for wires as he did so. There, on the back, was a small plastic box with a countdown dial on the front. It had six different coloured wires - two red, two yellow and two green – which were connected to a large square block of Semtex plastic explosive with a detonator stuck attached to it.

Commander Alfie got everybody well away as he started to check the wires for any electric current with his multimeter. He gently prised the wires apart as he tested each colour in turn. Only the two yellow wires had a current going through them from the plastic timer. He carefully bared the two wires with a scalpel and connected them (to keep the circuit complete) with a small length of jumper wire with a crocodile clip at each end.

With a steady hand, though shaking from excitement inside, Commander Alfie cut the two yellow wires below the clips with his pliers. The timer kept running although it was disarmed. He then cut all the other wires and gently slid the detonator out from the Semtex.

Commander Alfie looked at the timer and saw that he still

had twenty minutes to go before it would have exploded at eleven o clock. But twenty minutes was close enough for him!

He went back to the office, were the man had been identified by his photo as a wanted terrorist. He still refused to talk and tell the officers questioning him who his accomplices were and about his organisation. Commander Alfie asked to see the officer who was questioning the terrorist, as he had a plan.

The stationmaster was asked to change the large station clock back to a quarter to eleven before the terrorist was led outside to the bus parking area and asked which bus he had put the bomb on. He still refused to talk so Commander Alfie told him that as the bomb couldn't be found he was going to handcuff him to the handrail at the back of one of the Double Decker buses until he talked or it blew up! He handcuffed the terrorist to a bus that he had apparently picked out at random. It was, of course, the bus that had had the bomb on it that Commander Alfie had disarmed, but the terrorist didn't know that it had been found.

"You can't leave me here! What about my human rights?" screamed the now desperate terrorist, as they handcuffed him to the bus and started to walk away.

"Tell us everything and we will take you back to the Yard," said Commander Alfie.

"If you change your mind and decide to talk, just wave. We are going to get behind that thick wall over there to wait. Goodbye."

Looking at his watch, Alfie said loudly. "Okay men. Stand well back as it is five to eleven!"

The terrorist looked at the large station clock and started to wave and scream as he pulled wildly at the handcuffs chaining him to the bus. Then he cracked and decided to tell them everything. He really wanted to get away from the bus that he thought was about to explode!

"It's in this bus! Under that panel," he screamed and he

started to tell the police all they wanted to know. In those five minutes before eleven o clock the police learnt enough about his contacts and organisation to arrest all of its members.

The rest of the senior policemen back at New Scotland Yard congratulated Commander Alfie - although they thought it was a bit of a tough way to get information! But maybe giving the terrorist a taste of his own medicine, thinking he was about to be blown up, taught him a lesson.

Commander Alfie went back to his office and had just started to type out his report, when there was a knock at the door.

"Morning farmer, its cockcrow," said an Inspector at New Scotland Yard. Commander Alfie looked puzzled.

"I said good morning farmer, it's cockcrow," repeated Alfie's Dad, pulling his covers back. "Time for good young farm-workers to get up."

Alfie waited for his father to leave the room before looking under his pillow. He found a small piece of green wire with a crocodile clip on each end and a roll of insulation tape. He put them in his jean pocket and quickly got washed and dressed in his old clothes ready for the farm.

Chapter Sixteen
Souls Saved

Alfie ate a large bowl of cornflakes and had an egg on toast for his breakfast. Then he readied himself for a day on the farm, pulling on his new Wellingtons, a t-shirt and pair of old jeans. He said goodbye to a very disappointed Eddie and left for Top End farm.

"Morning, young Alfie!" said Farmer Appleton. "Nice to see a young man who can get up early in the morning."

That morning was spent feeding the cattle, pigs and calves. Alfie liked mixing the milk and putting it into buckets to feed the calves. They sucked his fingers as they looked for more milk. He learnt how to fill the hay nets and check the animals to make sure they were well.

Alfie was pleased to sit down at lunchtime and have some lunch with the farmer. It was a nice stew with carrots and potatoes in it. "Don't suppose that you get rabbit stew at home?" said Farmer Appleton's wife. Alfie had really been enjoying it till then. He kept thinking of fluffy bunnies! He was glad he had almost finished before she told him what it was.

Still, the apple crumble and custard for dessert was great.

That afternoon Alfie helped the farmer get his combine ready to cut his fields of wheat. He tightened pulleys with a spanner and pumped grease into the bearings.

The farmer sharpened his cutter bar blades with a small grinder. "There, nice and sharp ready to start," said Farmer Appleton. Alfie used the compressor to blow up the tyres and check the pressures. He filled the huge fuel tank with diesel and then dipped the oil. They were ready for harvest.

Farmer Appleton climbed into the combine's air-conditioned cab, turned the ignition key and nothing happened. "Won't start. No power," he said briefly, being a man of few words.

Alfie and Farmer Appleton started to check the wires. The farmer started at the battery and Alfie followed the cabling in the cab. "Be blowed if I can see anything wrong up here." said Farmer Appleton. "Suppose I had better call out the mechanic - though he's not cheap at harvest time."

Alfie suddenly saw the problem. It was a small wire to the ignition switch that was chewed apart. "Look here, I think I've found the trouble… and I think I know how to fix it."

Alfie reached in his pocket and took out the wire with a crocodile clip on each end; he joined the two chewed ends with the wire and taped over the joins with some insulation tape. The farmer marvelled at his ingenuity as the lights came on and the engine burst into life when the starter button was pressed. "Well done Alfie. I think you deserve a bonus on your first day!"

Mrs Appleton drove the tractor and corn trailer as the combine cut the champion wheat crop. Alfie was allowed to sit in the combines cab as the crop was cut. The air conditioning was lovely and cool. It was soon five o'clock and Alfie's Mum had come to see what her lad was up to. She found Alfie sitting by the side of the field with the Appleton's eating a harvest tea. She joined them for a cup of tea and a slice of fruitcake, as Farmer Appleton told them how Alfie had got the combine started after mice had chewed a wire through.

"He is pretty inventive!" said his mother proudly. "Just like his dad."

The field was almost finished when a contractor arrived to bale the straw. He had a huge machine that picked the straw up and rolled it into the big round bales in plastic wrapping, which Alfie had used to feed the cattle.

The weather started to change as the last of the wheat was tipped up in the grain store. The thunderclouds of a summer storm started to gather and the wind started to get stronger as the contractor worked furiously to beat the forthcoming rain. He was just wrapping the last bale at eight o'clock that night when the heavens opened. The rain poured down in torrents.

Farmer Appleton drove Alfie and his Mum home in his Land Rover and as he dropped them off he pushed an envelope into Alfie's top pocket. "Well done lad… and a little bonus for you." he said. "I won't need you tomorrow because of this rain, but if you hadn't helped fix the combine, we would have lost the crop!"

"Thank you Farmer Appleton. And, if next time you need a lot of help, I can bring my friend William," suggested Alfie. The Farmer nodded and said he would bear it in mind.

Alfie dashed into the house out of the rain and held the door open for his Mum.

Eddie met Alfie, jumped up him, and gave him a big lick.

"He's pleased to see you," said his Dad.

"And I'm pleased to see him! I didn't know it was such hard work being a farmer," said Alfie, exhausted.

Alfie got ready for bed and his Mum picked up his clothes to put them in the washing machine. Alfie just rescued the envelope that Farmer Appleton had given him before his Mum closed the washing machine door.

He opened the envelope to find that it had got thirty pounds in it - one twenty and two five-pound notes. He got his savings book out and asked his Dad to put twenty-five pounds in the bank for him, deciding to keep one of the fivers for buying something new.

Eddie jumped on the bed as a loud rumble of thunder cracked outside. He was cuddled by Alfie, who soon started to drift off to sleep after his busy day.

That night the storm thundered away and lightning streaks flashed across the sky. The rain beat on Alfie's bedroom window like a drum roll.

Coxswain Alfie looked at the barometer on his cottage wall. It was dropping lower and lower as the storm developed and got stronger. He looked out of the window and could barely see the harbour through the rain. The wind was howling, shutters were slamming and the loose wires on the masts of the moored yachts were clattering and dinging. He had just sat down in his chair to watch television when his telephone rang and his bleeper sounded. Coxswain Alfie jumped up and ran out the door pulling his coat on.

He raced down the cobbled streets towards the Lifeboat House. He prided himself that he was always the first to get to the station when the call went out. The other five volunteer lifeboat men were all running down the street now.

Coxswain Alfie had just spoken to the coastguard to find out about the distress call. It was a yacht in trouble called "*The Dizzy Maid*". A family was on board and the storm had whipped up large waves that had broken the yacht's front window. The water was getting in and the engine was flooded. The navigation aids had failed and the family crew weren't sure of their position. They could see lights of houses way off to their port and they knew that they were in close proximity to some rocks.

All the six lifeboat men quickly pulled their bright orange waterproof survival suits on and boarded *The Lord Wharley* lifeboat. The engines roared into life as Coxswain Alfie gave the order for the station man to hit the chains that retained the boat with a sledgehammer. The chain parted and *The Lord Wharley* thundered down the slipway into the teeth of the gale – exactly seven minutes after the bleepers first went off!

The water whooshed up over the bows as the boat hit the water. The throttles were opened wide as Coxswain Alfie manned the helm. They headed, flat out with all lights blazing, into the rain, wind and darkness; towards the point where Coxswain Alfie thought that the yacht might be found.

"Dizzy Maid! Dizzy Maid! This is lifeboat, *The Lord*

Wharley," said Coxswain Alfie into his radio. "Are you receiving? Over."

"*Lord Wharley, Lord Wharley*. This is *The Dizzy Maid*. We see your lights… North North East of us… we are taking in…" a voice crackled over the radio before fizzing out.

"The signals gone Coxswain! They must be sinking!" shouted the radio operator, twiddling the nobs to see if he could pick up another signal.

"Still can't see them on the radar!" called the first mate, scanning his screen.

Coxswain Alfie ordered a parachute flare to be fired towards South-South West. The flare lit up the sea all around as they strained their eyes through the lifeboats windows.

"There! A yacht's mast! Off to the starboard… no lights visible and it seems to be well down on the bows," called Look-Out.

Coxswain Alfie eased the throttles back as he drew nearer. *The Dizzy Maid* was swaying wildly in the gale and he could now see a small torch being waved by the crew. He battled the wind and waves so he could approach from down wind, so that *The Dizzy Maid* would drift towards *The Lord Wharley*. The two boats touched with a bang on the fenders and a lifeboat man scrambled onto *The Dizzy Maid's* deck with a rope. Working swiftly and struggling against the elements, the yacht's crew were carefully helped onto the lifeboat. One of the rescued family was only about three years old!

The father wanted Coxswain Alfie to save *The Dizzy Maid*.

"Lives first and foremost," instructed Coxswain Alfie sternly. "The yacht comes second!"

The rescued family were given foil blankets and put safely below. Then efforts to save the yacht began. A small portable pump was roped securely to *The Dizzy Maid's* deck and the petrol engine burst into life. A stream of water issued out of the pumps drainage pipe. The lifeboat crew got back on *The Lord Wharley* and took the yacht in tow. The two 500 horse-

power engines pushed *The Lord Wharley* and *The Dizzy Maid* at an easy pace back towards harbour.

The waves were still crashing against the boat's sides as they reached the safety of the harbour walls. An ambulance was waiting on the quayside, alerted by the radio operator. The lifeboat drew alongside the sheltered jetty and the very grateful yacht's family disembarked.

The Lord Wharley was refuelled and the duty mechanic checked her engines over in readiness for her to go out again. *The Dizzy Maid* was tied up on a quayside mooring.

Coxswain Alfie went back to his cottage and sat down in front of a warm log fire. He filled the ship's log in with all the rescue details. He always got great satisfaction from filling in the column for "Souls Saved".

Four, he wrote, as he dozed off in his chair.

Chapter Seventeen
The Upside-Down Magazine

The bleeper sounded and Alfie reached out of bed to turn his alarm off. He looked at the time. It was seven o'clock. He went to turn over, decided to stay in bed a bit longer in bed as Farmer Appleton didn't need him today. Sleepily, he reached under his pillow and found a used parachute flare cartridge.

Eddie decided that it was time to get up so he jumped on Alfie then stood behind the door in the opening and looked round the door. "All right Eddie, you win, I'll let you out in the garden," said Alfie.

His Dad was up and shaving in the bathroom. "Hey Alfie, if you aren't working today, why not put the money in the bank yourself?"

"Yes Dad, I will," said Alfie, liking the idea of a trip to the bank and shops.

After breakfast Alfie took Eddie with him, as a Guard Dog, to take the twenty-five pounds to the bank. All the way to the bank Alfie was looking out for bandits or highwaymen. Eddie caught on and looked round just as anxiously - for cats!

They reached the bank. Alfie tied Eddie up outside, explaining he would be back in a minute. Alfie proudly paid the wages into the cashier who took Alfie's passbook and credited the money to his account. Alfie carefully checked the adding up and agreed the total before he left the bank.

As he left, Alfie noticed a nervous looking man parked across the street on a double yellow line. He was smoking a cigarette, pretending to read a magazine but Alfie noticed it was upside down and the car's engine was running. A heap of fag ends lay on the road below the driver's door. Alfie thought that the man was waiting for something, but what?

He went next door to the newsagents, leaving Eddie up outside as he went in and spent some of his remaining fiver on a magazine and some sweets. When he came out, he observed the parked car was still there.

Alfie spotted a policeman was heading towards the newsagents, so Alfie went up to him and pointed out the suspicious parked car with the man in it.

The policeman went into the newsagents and peered through the window so he couldn't be seen, and he radioed headquarters for a number plate check. A few minutes later it was confirmed that the car was falsely registered for that make, type and colour. The policeman called for the Area Car to back him up, and he told Alfie to collect Eddie from outside and to stay inside the shop.

Just as the policeman went to challenge the driver a loud alarm bell started to ring from inside the bank next door. Two men with stockings over their heads dashed out towards the car. It was a robbery!

The policeman wrestled one of the robbers to the ground and a struggle took place. The other robber threw a bag of money into the back of the car and went to help his mate who was wrestling with the policeman.

Alfie and the shopkeeper dashed out to help. Eddie went with them. Soon the shopkeeper, two robbers and the policeman were rolling on the ground. The car driver got out to help his mates, not seeing Alfie sneak around. Alfie reached inside the car's open window and performed his favourite trick of grabbing the ignition keys.

The driver grabbed Alfie by the scruff of the neck to get the keys back, but Alfie accidentally dropped the keys down a drain grid. The furious driver pulled his arm back to lay a heavy punch on Alfie when Eddie launched himself at the driver's

arm and sunk his teeth in. The man howled with pain just as the area police car screeched to a halt and two more policemen suddenly evened up the odds.

The robbers were overpowered and arrested and the money was returned to the bank.

The policemen stood around taking down statements from everyone. Alfie was glowing with pride, although the policeman also told him sternly, "I told you to stay in the shop. You could have been seriously hurt. If that guy had punched you, he would have laid you out for a week as he was a big guy – and they could have had guns."

Alfie looked sheepish, and the policeman patted him on the back. "You did well to spot the man in the beginning, however. Well done."

The bank manager invited Alfie and Eddie into his office and ordered in a cup of tea and doughnuts for them.

"You were very brave," said Mr Morden the bank manager. "We nearly lost twenty thousand pounds today. The police said that it was your information that led to the robbers being found out. They are a well-known gang, and the bank is offering a reward for their capture. I believe it's about ten percent of the recovered value, and is awarded after the case has come to court."

'Ten percent? Ten percent?' thought Alfie, as he tried to work out what ten percent of twenty thousand pounds was. "That's two thousand pounds reward!" he gasped.

Alfie and Eddie tucked into another doughnut each as the manager said that it would be best to keep quiet about Alfie's involvement in foiling the robbery. He was worried that crooks could read the papers and try to get even.

Alfie was walking home when he remembered that he had left his sweets and magazine in the shop. He ran back for them, realising that he was now late for his lunch at home. The shopkeeper had saved the sweets and magazine for him, and gave him a large bunch of flowers for his Mum. Alfie thanked him and walked back with Eddie to Acacia Drive.

Alfie's mum was looking out for him as he came into view. She immediately became suspicious when she saw the flowers. "Is this to stop me being angry because you are late?" she asked him sternly. Alfie told her all about the robbery and how he had helped the policeman to foil it.

"Good grief!" she said. "Can't you ever go out without something happening?"

Chapter Eighteen
The Air-Scrubber

Alfie sat down to eat his ham and cheese salad lunch. Eddie quickly gobbled his own lunch down and sat down by Alfie's side. "Don't give him any of your lunch as he's fat enough already," said Alfie's Mum. Then she went straight to Eddie's snack cupboard and gave him a chew bone.

"Oh, and William called earlier for you. I told him you would phone him back when you got back."

Alfie finished the salad and called William. "William's coming round in five minutes, Mum," said Alfie.

Soon the doorbell rang and it was William. "Hello Alfie. Guess what, my uncle Ted the inventor is back and he wants to see us; let's take him those plans you have," suggested William.

Alfie went to the drawer under his bed and took out the plans and the silver button.

Uncle Ted was in his workshop when they arrived and William's aunt showed them where he was.

"You must be Alfie?" said Uncle Ted. "I am very glad that you and William saved me from being burgled."

"Grace helped as well," said Alfie, "but she's working at the beach café today."

"Well, as a reward, I'm going to take you all out soon for a day at Alton Towers; we can go on the train."

"That's great thanks," said the two boys excitedly.

Uncle Ted noticed the plans rolled up under Alfie's arm. "We brought them for you to have a look at and to see if you could make it?" said William.

Uncle Ted opened the plans out on the table and stared at them. "I don't understand the writing but I can see the principle involved," he said.

Alfie held the silver button in his pocket and leant over, lightly touching Uncle Ted's shoulder as if he were also looking. The button's power transferred and Uncle Ted suddenly started to write furiously on the plan with a pencil.

"I can see it all now! It's wonderful!" he said. "Let's make a scaled down prototype to see if it works."

The two boys helped to cut out various metal sections and Uncle Ted drilled and joined them together. Uncle Ted went searching amongst the shelves at the back of the workshop and came back with an old extractor fan unit. He bolted it in the frame and then connected a cable to it. He then filled an old water tank with barbeque charcoal and sand.

He then connected water pipes, a spray head and an old pressure washer pump.

It was getting late so William's aunt rang their mothers and she she would give them some tea, after which the boys said goodbye and left for home. They left Uncle Ted in his workshop, working furiously on a control circuit board for the ionizer on the Air Scrubber. He didn't really notice them leaving.

When Alfie got home, it was very late. As he got into his pyjamas, he told his Dad all about the robbery and how Mr Morden the bank manager had said there would be a large reward.

"Enough to take us on a special holiday again!" said Alfie.

"New York would be nice," suggested his Mum. "Especially a trip to Tiffany's, the jewellers, with your father and his credit card for a small diamond memento."

"I want to go up the Empire State building and see the "Intrepid" aircraft carrier and museum and go on the ferry to The Statue of Liberty," said Alfie.

"In that case I hope it's a very big reward to cope with all that!" said his Dad.

"Come on Alfie – it's time to get into bed," said his Mum, pulling back the duvet for him to clamber in. "And if we do go to New York, can we please not have any adventures?"

"That's not up to me, is it?" said Alfie, snuggling down into his bed. "We'll just have to wait and see!"